Earl the Vampire

Sean Michael Welch

A SAMUEL FRENCH ACTING EDITION

SAMUEL FRENCH

FOUNDED 1830

SAMUELFRENCH.COM
SAMUELFRENCH-LONDON.CO.UK

FOR PRODUCTION ENQUIRIES

UNITED STATES AND CANADA

Info@SamuelFrench.com

1-866-598-8449

UNITED KINGDOM AND EUROPE

Theatre@SamuelFrench-London.co.uk

020-7255-4302

Each title is subject to availability from Samuel French, depending upon country of performance. Please be aware that *EARL THE VAMPIRE* may not be licensed by Samuel French in your territory. Professional and amateur producers should contact the nearest Samuel French office or licensing partner to verify availability.

MUSIC USE NOTE

Licensees are solely responsible for obtaining formal written permission from copyright owners to use copyrighted music in the performance of this play and are strongly cautioned to do so. If no such permission is obtained by the licensee, then the licensee must use only original music that the licensee owns and controls. Licensees are solely responsible and liable for all music clearances and shall indemnify the copyright owners of the play(s) and their licensing agent, Samuel French, against any costs, expenses, losses and liabilities arising from the use of music by licensees. Please contact the appropriate music licensing authority in your territory for the rights to any incidental music.

IMPORTANT BILLING AND CREDIT REQUIREMENTS

If you have obtained performance rights to this title, please refer to your licensing agreement for important billing and credit requirements.

EARL THE VAMPIRE was first performed in its original form on February 13, 1998, at the University of Michigan Flint's Black Box Theatre. The performance was directed by Sean Michael Welch, with sets by Marie L. Glenn, costumes by Jennifer L. Rudolph, lighting by Andrew Florida, and props by Michelle Abbot. The Production Stage Manager was Michele Burch. The cast was as follows:

EARL (LORD EVIDO) .... Gregory Nicolai
ETHAN .... Jon Kelley
HAMPTON .... Eric Miller
SHANA..Jennifer L. Rudolph
DANIEL...Jason Bretzlaff
CANDY, TRESA .... Jennifer Wheeler
PEACHES/GRETCHEN...........................Marie L. Glenn
OLIVE/LUCINA .... Alicia J. Lamb
CHRISTY BANKS....................................E. J. Borrego
VANRUEGEN/CAMERA MAN/MAN WITH SUMMONS . . .Jonathan Grenay
DETECTIVE BILLS .... Paul Schutt
DETECTIVE SHARP ....Joseph Alberts
THE HUNTER....................................Heath Blackerby
VOICE OF BRADY LENNOX......................... William Irwin

EARL THE VAMPIRE was performed on April 9, 1999 at the Kennedy Center for the American College Theatre Festival. The performance was directed by Sean Michael Welch, with sets by Marie L. Glenn and Bert Scott, costume design by Jennifer L. Rudolph, lighting by Andrew Florida and Amir Hasan, props by Michelle Abbot and Jennifer Wheeler, and music and sound by Rob Hill, Jason Hurley, and Matthew Payne. The Production Stage Manager was Michele Burch. The cast was as follows:

EARL (LORD EVIDO) .... Gregory Nicolai
ETHAN .... Jon Kelley
HAMPTON .... Eric Miller
SHANA..Jennifer L. Rudolph
DANIEL...Jason Bretzlaff
VANRUEGEN/CAMERAMAN/MAN WITH SUMMONS. . . .Jonathan Grenay
THE HUNTER......................................Jason Hurley
CHRISTY BANKS................................ Christine Rickard
DETECTIVE BILLS .... Paul Schutt
DETECTIVE SHARP ....Joseph Alberts
LUCINA...Shelly Dunning
TRESA .... Jennifer Wheeler
GRETCHEN.....................................Marie L. Glenn
VOICE OF BRADY LENNOX......................... William Irwin

CHARACTERS

The Family

EARL (LORD EVIDO) – Became a vampire in his mid to late 20s. Reclusive, sullen and mysterious.

ETHAN – Became a vampire in his mid to late 20s. Controlled and easy going. The family's patriarch.

HAMPTON – Became a vampire in his early 20s. Vain, self-absorbed and driven.

SHANA – Became a vampire in late teens to early 20s. Foul-tempered, yet loving. The family's matriarch.

DANIEL – Became a vampire in his mid to late teens. Boyish, energetic, but somewhat slow.

The Outsiders

CHRISTY BANKS – Mid to late 20s. A television interviewer. Overly spirited and anxious to prove herself.

BRADY LENNOX – Late 30s to early 40s. A local television talk show host. Loud and boisterous.

VANRUEGEN – Late 20s to early 30s. A government agent. Fast-talking, fast-thinking.

DETECTIVE BILLS – Mid to late 30s. A police detective. All business and by-the-book.

DETECTIVE SHARP – Early to mid 30s. A police detective. Comparable to his partner Bills, but with a slight edge.

THE HUNTER – Late 30s to early 40s. A vampire hunter. Rugged and mean.

The Representatives

GRETCHEN – Became a vampire in her late 20s to early 30s. Politically-minded and exceedingly focused.

LUCINA – Became a vampire in her early to mid 20s. Sexy and flirtatious.

TRESA – Became a vampire in her late teens to early 20s. Youthful and brash.

*The **CAMERAMAN** and the **MAN WITH SUMMONS** to be played by the same actor as **VANRUEGEN**.

For Tamara

ACT I

Scene One

(A normal living room, dim lighting. A shadowy figure, **EARL THE VAMPIRE**, *lurks among the darkness. An organ plays a dirge. Enter* **ETHAN** *from hallway.)*

ETHAN. Dammit, Earl! Would you stop...lurking? And for Christ's sake, turn on that light.

*(***ETHAN*** exits to the kitchen.)*

EARL. I am not Earl.

*(***ETHAN*** enters with a newspaper and a cup of coffee.)*

ETHAN. Sorry...Lord Evido, would you please turn on the light?

*(***EARL*** turns on the light. ***ETHAN*** sits in the recliner and starts reading. An alarm sounds and then is turned off. ***EARL*** takes his place standing in the corner of the room. Enter* **HAMPTON** *from bedroom.)*

HAMPTON. Who did the shopping this week? Was it Shana? Because I made it clear to her that we were running low on shampoo. I just want to be able to go out at night and not feel like my hair is – like it sticks to my head and sometimes it itches, and I can't do *anything* because I'm too busy being distracted by my hair. But does anyone care? No. Because no one has the oily hair problem except me. You can just throw a baseball cap on and you're fine. I'm not a hat person.

ETHAN. Did you check under the sink?

*(***HAMPTON*** hesitates, then exits into hallway. ***HAMPTON*** then re-enters.)*

HAMPTON. Shana grabbed the bathroom before I could get back. We should have a bigger house. One with *two* bathrooms.

ETHAN. Are you in line for a promotion at work?

HAMPTON. Is the coffee on? Hey, Earl, will you grab me a cup if I call you Lord Evido?

EARL. No.

(HAMPTON *exits to kitchen.*)

ETHAN. Speaking of work, you go in tonight?

(HAMPTON *returns with a cup of coffee.*)

HAMPTON. What say?

(ETHAN, *almost habitually, hands* HAMPTON *the entertainment section.* HAMPTON *sits on the couch.*)

God, would you look at this? Another movie, another forty million dollar paycheck.

ETHAN. Tonight's Tuesday, isn't it? Don't you work?

HAMPTON. No, I quit. I want forty million dollars. Then we would have two bathrooms. No, better yet, five. One for each of us.

ETHAN. Again you quit?

(*Enter* SHANA *from hallway.*)

HAMPTON. My boss was a putz.

SHANA. Hampton, dear, do you have to leave your socks soaking in the sink?

HAMPTON. They had bloodstains on'em.

ETHAN. Your boss "was" a putz?

SHANA. It's disgusting. They don't have to soak all day, just use some bleach and hot water.

ETHAN. What do you mean "was"?

HAMPTON. I forgot about them, okay?

SHANA. Go get your socks out of the sink! I wanna brush my teeth!

ETHAN. What did you do?

HAMPTON. You seem to already have an idea.

ETHAN. Do you not think about these things?

HAMPTON. Of course I do. But then I go *eh* and forget about it.

ETHAN. That was your *only* source of income.

SHANA. Socks. Sink. Out.

HAMPTON. *You* don't have a job right now.

ETHAN. I'm collecting unemployment.

SHANA. Socks.

HAMPTON. Then I'll collect unemployment.

SHANA. Now. Socks now.

ETHAN. One: You have to be *fired* or *laid-off* from a job in order to collect. Two: you have to manage to keep a job more than *two weeks* in order to collect.

SHANA. *(grabbing* **HAMPTON** *by the ear)* GET YOUR FUCKING SOCKS OUT OF THE SINK!

(Exit **HAMPTON** *to hallway followed by* **SHANA.** *The alarm sounds.* **ETHAN** *lifts up the lid of the coffin table, reaches into it, turning the alarm off.)*

ETHAN. Are you going to keep hitting that snooze bar all night, Danny?

DANIEL. *(getting out of coffin)* Sorry. I didn't sleep very well. I kept having nightmares.

ETHAN. Probably something you ate.

*(***SHANA** *enters.)*

SHANA. You know, ever since Hampton found out that one talk show host was a vampire, he's been even more impossible to live with. That guy with the nose...

ETHAN. Oh, him. Yeah, I love that guy.

SHANA. *(to* **DANIEL***)* Morning, sweetie. Morning, Evido.

DANIEL. Do we have anything to eat?

ETHAN. Nothing substantial. Maybe a breast, or a thigh... or a hand.

*(***ETHAN** *pulls out a little yellow memo pad and a pen, scribbles on it.)*

SHANA. Are you going out tonight, Evido? Could you bring something back with you? I don't think I'm going to go out tonight. I want to clean the kitchen. It's getting out of hand.

EARL. As you wish.

SHANA. See? He's polite. He knows how to treat a lady, unlike some people.

ETHAN. Hey, I just woke up. *(beat)* Here.

*(***ETHAN*** *hands* ***SHANA*** *a piece of yellow memo paper.)*

SHANA. Not you, sweetie. I'm talking about the prick in the bathroom, who is, as we speak, taking a shower and *not* getting his socks out of the sink. I'm going to flush the toilet, and see how he likes that.

*(***SHANA*** *starts exiting to hallway.)*

ETHAN. That is so mean. I *love you.*

SHANA. *(looking at memo paper)* What's this?

ETHAN. Hampton is putting shampoo on the shopping list. For extra oily hair.

SHANA. Great. And, look, it's small enough to fit up Hampton's tight ass.

*(***SHANA*** *crumples the note in her hand and exits.)*

ETHAN. So, what's your schedule for tonight, Danny?

DANIEL. I don't know. Hampton is supposed to take me somewhere, I guess.

(offstage: toilet flush)

HAMPTON. *(responding to cold water)* AHHHHH! YOU BITCH! I HATE YOU!

*(***SHANA*** *enters.)*

SHANA. That was fun.

ETHAN. *(to* **DANIEL***)* Oh, yeah? Somewhere like where?

DANIEL. He wouldn't tell me. I think it's a secret.

SHANA. What are we talking about?

ETHAN. Hampton's taking Daniel on a field trip.

SHANA. Oh, yeah? To the zoo?

DANIEL. I like the zoo! I don't think he's taking me to the zoo, though.

ETHAN. Remember the last time *we* went to the zoo? What was that? Nineteen forty something?

SHANA. 1938. Do you remember?

ETHAN. *(slightly aroused)* You kidding? I still have the scars on my back.

DANIEL. I like the monkeys. They're my favorite.

EARL. I am leaving. I wish you all a good evening.

(*EARL exits through the kitchen.*)

SHANA. Night, babe.

DANIEL. I had a weird dream last night.

ETHAN. I dreamt about sweaters. I don't know why. Me in a room surrounded by sweaters.

SHANA. You have a very boring dreamlife.

(*HAMPTON enters talking into his tape recorder.*)

HAMPTON. No one ever said that creatures of night couldn't have a few yuks to pass the time. All good fun. *(Turns recorder off. To SHANA.)* You are SO FUCKING FUNNY! I love that flush the toilet so the shower gets wicked cold gag! *(beat)* You gonna take a shower before we go, Daniel?

DANIEL. No, I'm okay.

HAMPTON. Take a shower before we go, Daniel.

DANIEL. Yeah, okay.

(*DANIEL exits to bedroom area.*)

ETHAN. What's up with the recorder? I'm curious.

HAMPTON. It's my memoirs, okay? I'm writing a book.

(*Beat. ETHAN and SHANA laugh.*)

HAMPTON. It's a great idea. The life of a vampire? That's best-selling gold right there.

SHANA. Like you'll ever finish it. Like you ever finish *anything.*

HAMPTON. Oh, I finish things. Believe me.

SHANA. Like your stamp collection?

HAMPTON. That was a hobby. This is a project.

ETHAN: Where are you and Daniel going that he needs to take a shower?

SHANA. Is it the zoo?

HAMPTON. Hey, how come we don't own a hair dryer?

ETHAN. I don't know, I never asked.

HAMPTON. We could use a good hair dryer. With three speeds. Settings. Whatever you call'em.

ETHAN. If you want a hair dryer, go *buy* a hair dryer. Oh, wait…you don't have a job. Huh.

HAMPTON. Can I –

ETHAN. And don't put it on the shopping list.

HAMPTON. But air-drying makes it all…if I leave it too long it gets hard to comb.

ETHAN. Then maybe you need a better comb. With three speeds. Settings. Whatever.

(**SHANA** *exits to kitchen.*)

HAMPTON. You just want me to have hard to comb hair.

ETHAN. Yes, Hampton. The only joy I can find in life anymore is making sure that you have hard to comb hair. Gingivitis would be a coup, so dental floss is on the hit list as well. Time permitting, embarrassing body odor.

HAMPTON. Are you insinuating something? (*smelling armpit*) Do I smell? Where's my Old Spice?

(**HAMPTON** *exits to bedroom area.* **ETHAN** *returns to reading the paper. Enter* **DANIEL.**)

ETHAN. Quick shower.

DANIEL. I just rubbed myself with the deodorant. Don't tell, okay?

ETHAN. Not me. (*pause*) Something on your mind, kiddo?

DANIEL. Do you want to hear about my dream?

ETHAN. Sure, what the hell.

DANIEL. *(beat)* Okay, so…I fell asleep, right? And then, I was dangling from a rope, by my ankles…and below me, it was all black. And above me was black too. The rope sort of disappeared, so I couldn't see what it was hanging onto, you know? And all around me…like a… like it was a well or something…all circular. But the walls were made up of all these mouths, and I couldn't make out what they were saying, because they were all talking and screaming at once. I tried to lift myself up and untie my ankles, but then I fell. And then I woke up and hit the snooze bar. It was spooky.

ETHAN. Much more interesting than being in a room of sweaters, though. *(beat)* You have no idea where Hampton's taking you?

DANIEL. No. I kinda wish it was the zoo now, though. I like the monkeys.

(Enter SHANA *carrying a bloody arm.)*

SHANA. Daniel? What have I told you about leaving food out? This is why we have a refrigerator. Now I have to throw it out.

DANIEL. I'm sorry, Shana.

SHANA. Just think about it next time.

*(*SHANA *puts the arm back into the kitchen.)*

DANIEL. I will.

*(*HAMPTON *enters.)*

HAMPTON. Let's go, Daniel, I smell good.

*(*HAMPTON *and* DANIEL *head for the front door.)*

SHANA. So, where you two boys headed tonight?

HAMPTON. To the zoo, okay?

DANIEL. Really? I was right?

HAMPTON. We're not going to the zoo, Daniel.

DANIEL. But you said –

HAMPTON. The zoo is *closed*, Daniel.

DANIEL. The zoo is always closed when we go. It's not open at night.

(Enter **EARL** *from kitchen.)*

ETHAN. That was quick. Did you find a runaway in the backyard?

EARL. It is not a good hour to feed. Something in the wind...

HAMPTON. You're a nut, Earl. I love ya. Let's go, Danny.

ETHAN. Have fun at the zoo.

HAMPTON. We're not going to the zoo!

DANIEL. I like the zoo.

HAMPTON. *(pause)* We'll go to the zoo after our appointment.

(**DANIEL** *exits gleefully through the front door, followed by* **HAMPTON**.)

SHANA. Hampton was kinda sweet just then. Gonna mark this day down on the calendar.

ETHAN. We'll celebrate with dinner and balloons.

EARL. They should not have gone. This hour of night is poised to bring harm.

Scene Two

(Spotlight up on **VANRUEGEN.***)*

VANRUEGEN. Vampires kill humans to survive. They n.
the blood of others. They kill because it is necessary.
They do not discriminate. They have no religion. They
have no faith. Blood is necessary to them. The blood
of humans. It gives them power. They kill because it is
pleasurable. They care nothing for humans. They are
not human. They exist to promote evil. They *are* evil.
There is no sense of decency within them. There is no
mercy. They have no emotions. They have no loyalty.
They have no sense of family. They have no capacity
for compassion…morality…love.

Scene Three

(SHANA is flipping through channels. EARL stands in the corner.)

SHANA. God, remember when there used to be only like four channels and something was always on? *(looks at EARL)* Look who I'm talking to. *(flipping channels)* Crap. Crap. Crap. Cr…

(SHANA gets a closer look at the TV. EARL comes closer.)

SHANA. Um…Ethan?

ETHAN. *(off)* I'm in the bathroom!

SHANA. ETHAN!

ETHAN. WILL YOU GIMME A MINUTE, PLEASE!?!

(The toilet flushes off.)

SHANA. I'm so serious right now!

(ETHAN enters from hallway.)

ETHAN. Are we out of air freshener?

SHANA. Look at this.

(ETHAN walks over to SHANA, looks at TV.)

ETHAN. Oh, yeah, that's Brady Lennox. *Never* watch him. Only so much I can learn about transvestites.

SHANA. Look who his guests are.

ETHAN. I would if he'd shut up for a moment –

SHANA. SHHHH!

(A moment. ETHAN sees what SHANA is referring to.)

ETHAN. No.

SHANA. This is…is this bad? I haven't decided yet.

ETHAN. That sonuvabitch. That stupid sonuvabitch!

SHANA. It could be bad. No, it's not, it's fine. I mean, Hampton and Daniel are on TV but…yeah, it's not like…you know?

ETHAN. Yeah. No you're right. I mean, it's a talk show. They're just talking. No big deal.

SHANA. I was really hoping you'd say that. I'm gonna finish with the dishes. Break time's over.

(**SHANA** *exits to kitchen.*)

ETHAN. Still like to know what he's trying to prove, though.

EARL. This is unacceptable.

ETHAN. Relax. I mean, yeah, he's on TV, but it's local and...I mean, what does he expect...? *(pause)* Oh, no. Oh, no no no. Don't you do it, Hampton! Don't you fucking do it! *(pause)* Oh, Christ, you fucking did it! SHANA!

(**SHANA** *enters.*)

SHANA. Did he flex his fangs? Big deal –

ETHAN. He bled a sheep.

SHANA. *(beat) No,* he *didn't.* What happened to the picture?

ETHAN. They cut to commercial before he could finish. Jesus Christ, he drained a sheep! That little –

SHANA. Okay, let's think about this...*(pause)* No, sorry, I got nothin'.

EARL. I hunger.

ETHAN. There's a few things in the fridge. Help yourself.

EARL. I do not hunt refrigerators.

ETHAN. I'm sorry, but after this? Make do with what we have here. If it'll help I can put limbs on a string and drag them around the room for you.

SHANA. So, what are you going to do?

ETHAN. I don't know, I don't...yes, I do. I'm going to rip his fangs out of his head.

SHANA. You're overreacting. I mean, sure, he sucked the blood out of the sheep, but...at best people won't think he's a vampire, they'll just ask if he'd like to join their freakshow. Right?

ETHAN. I'm going to use them for letter openers.

SHANA. Listen to me. This month: vampires. Next month? A celebrity kills a hooker. It's a footnote because deep deep down, humans won't let themselves believe that we exist. Because if we exist, then it means that they are not in charge of the world anymore. And they cannot even *fathom* that concept.

(a moment)

EARL. I hunger.
ETHAN. I know.

Scene Four

(Enter **DANIEL** *and* **HAMPTON***. As they walk along, three black cloaked and hooded women (***GRETCHEN***, ***LUCINA***, and* **TRESA***) enter around them.)*

DANIEL. The zoo's *that* way.

HAMPTON. I know, I just wanna hit the bar first. Wanna get the taste of sheep blood…*(notices the hooded figures)* outta my mouth – can I help you?

GRETCHEN. Hello, Hampton.

LUCINA. We've been waiting for you.

GRETCHEN. We have common interests.

HAMPTON. Uh-huh. *(beat)* Okay, well, I'd be happy to talk it over with you sometime, so why don't you leave me a number and –

TRESA. The time is now.

HAMPTON. No, see I promised my little brother to take him to the zoo, and then I got a thing later –

GRETCHEN. We are ready.

(The three make a move closer to **HAMPTON***.)*

HAMPTON. Hey now, I'm not opposed to hitting women. Or Druids. And best not to think what we'd do to you after that.

LUCINA. Don't you know that you can't bite one of your own?

HAMPTON. *(beat)* Are you guys vampires? Did you see the show tonight?

TRESA. Yes.

HAMPTON. And…can you fill me in on which way you're leaning on that issue?

GRETCHEN. We wish to join you in your pursuits. To give a voice to all of our brethren.

HAMPTON. Well. That's good. *(beat)* Are the cloaks necessary, though? Kinda creepin' me out.

(A moment. The three huddle and confer. They remove their cloaks and let them drop to the floor.)

HAMPTON. *(referring to* **LUCINA***)* That's…so much better.

GRETCHEN. I am Gretchen, and these are Lucina and Tresa.

HAMPTON. Very nice.

GRETCHEN. We have been waiting so long for someone like you, brave enough to reveal your true self to the world. Because of such a public display, there's no way we can be ignored or exterminated in silence any longer.

TRESA. With support, we could take this a long way.

LUCINA. If we keep going in this direction, then there's no way it can be taken as a hoax. It will allow us to come out of the shadows and exist as a part of society.

GRETCHEN. But more importantly, a group with a political presence.

HAMPTON. So, you guys know other vampires?

GRETCHEN. Of course. Don't you?

HAMPTON. Well, yeah. Like…four.

LUCINA. And now you know three more.

(**GRETCHEN** *pulls out a business card and hands it to* **HAMPTON.***)*

GRETCHEN. Get a hold of us when you're ready.

(**GRETCHEN, TRESA,** *and* **LUCINA** *exit.* **DANIEL** *tugs on* **HAMPTON***'s sleeve.)*

DANIEL. Can we go to the zoo now?

Scene Five

(Spotlight on **DETECTIVE BILLS** *and* **DETECTIVE SHARP**.*)*

BILLS. It was three o'clock.

SHARP. AM.

BILLS. Two years ago.

SHARP. Approximately.

BILLS. We got the call.

SHARP. Strange happenings on Oak Street.

BILLS. We checked it out. A house…two-story…Victorian.

SHARP. Nice place. Very homey. But at three o'clock –

BILLS. Nothing's homey.

SHARP. We walked in.

BILLS. It was dark.

SHARP. Couldn't see a hand in front of your face.

BILLS. Yours or anyone else's.

SHARP. Lucky we had our flashlights.

BILLS. Three bodies in the dining room. What appeared to be bite marks on the neck, underarm, and leg areas. We knew something was wrong.

SHARP. Very wrong.

BILLS. So we searched the house. The den.

SHARP. The kitchen.

BILLS. The living room.

SHARP. I made a joke about it.

BILLS. I laughed.

SHARP. He did.

BILLS. Then upstairs. The hallway.

SHARP. The guest room.

BILLS. The bathroom.

SHARP. The other guest room.

BILLS. In the master bedroom, in the corner, just finishing up, hovering over a dead body, naked, covered in blood, his eyes gleaming up at us...I said, "You see that?"

SHARP. And I said, "Yeah." And Bills said, "What's this look like?"

BILLS. And Sharp said, "Cannibal. Psycho. *Vampire.*" You read storybooks. You check out the occasional video. But you never think that one day you'll be seeing the real thing.

SHARP. It's like Godzilla bearing down on Tokyo.

BILLS. That unreal. It's like waking up from a dream and realizing that it's not a dream.

SHARP. We accessed the situation. We had a real live vampire on our hands.

BILLS. It had to be. But yet, it was...still unbelievable. It was...the experience of it was...

SHARP. Like sex.

BILLS. Only harsh and cruel.

SHARP. Like sex.

BILLS. I knew what evil was. At least I knew it up until that point. It was rapists. Pedophiles. Murderers. I knew what they were. But this was different.

SHARP. Because it wasn't real.

BILLS. Who could be this? Who could do this? Who would want this?

SHARP. Every day?

BILLS. A regular Joe?

SHARP. Choosing this?

BILLS. Not possible.

SHARP. Because vampirism is a choice.

BILLS. Always a choice, from what I gather.

SHARP. We had a lot of questions.

BILLS. But we're detectives, and there are no easy answers.

SHARP. And no easy questions.

BILLS. And even fewer easy answers to those not-so-easy questions.

SHARP. And even fewer questions for those easy answers.

BILLS. Stop it. *(beat)* So there we were. The three of us. In a room. Without a judge.

SHARP. Or a jury.

BILLS. So we made a decision.

SHARP. Shoot to kill.

BILLS. End the nightmare where it stood. No human being could have done this.

SHARP. Not even an insane one.

BILLS. The choice was clear.

SHARP. Our guns were ready.

BILLS. We fired.

SHARP. We fired a lot.

BILLS. And then…of course, we realized that bullets don't work so well on vampires.

SHARP. So we just ran.

Scene Six

(**SHANA** *is massaging* **ETHAN**'*s back.* **EARL** *stands in the corner.*)

SHANA. Is the urge to kill subsiding?

ETHAN. Nope. But it still feels good.

(*Enter* **HAMPTON** *and* **DANIEL.**)

SHANA. Uh-oh.

(**SHANA** *exits to kitchen.*)

DANIEL. We went to the zoo tonight! (*beat*) Are there any of those fingers left in the freezer?

(**DANIEL** *exits to kitchen.*)

HAMPTON. Hello, Ethan. (*to* **EARL**) Bela.

ETHAN. So, you took Daniel to the zoo, huh?

HAMPTON. Yeah, you know, the monkey thing.

(*Enter* **DANIEL** *with a bowl of blood and a finger to dunk it in.*)

ETHAN. So…guess what I saw on TV tonight?

HAMPTON. How many guesses do I get?

ETHAN. I was watching *The Brady Lennox Show.* They were doing a show on vampires. You know, whether or not vampires exist? They even had a couple of guests that said they were actual vampires and could prove it. Ate a sheep. Whatcha think about that?

HAMPTON. Wasn't it cool? That Brady's a helluva nice guy. He's a lot shorter in person –

ETHAN. Do you know what you did?

HAMPTON. Of course I did. I was there.

ETHAN. Yes, you and Danny were both there. I watched you telling the whole world –

HAMPTON. It's local programming –

ETHAN. All right fine, local programming. But how long do you think before this story breaks, do you think?

Hmm? Because you know what happens now? Exposure. Vulnerability. The madness of crowds. Thanks, Hampton. I appreciate it.

EARL. You have violated our sacred order.

ETHAN. Don't help me, Earl!

EARL. Evido.

ETHAN. Evido!

HAMPTON. You have to look at the big picture here. The time has come for us to stop hiding. Sign of the times, babe. It's time for us to stop catering to the mythology. It's time for us to stop being Hollywood stereotypes, and tell the truth once and for all. Jesus, Ethan, there were people in that audience that thought we would all be like Earl.

EARL. Evido.

HAMPTON. I don't care.

ETHAN. Hey, Shana! Where do you wanna move to?

SHANA. *(off)* Anywhere but France.

HAMPTON. Just picture it, Ethan. Imagine what this could lead to. The possibilities are endless.

ETHAN. How about Peru? We've never been to Peru!

SHANA. *(off)* Yes, we have!

HAMPTON. Yep, the ball is already starting to roll –

ETHAN. Oh, yeah? When?

HAMPTON. It's all coming into focus –

SHANA. *(off)* Around 1903.

ETHAN. Did I like it?

HAMPTON. It's first and ten on the nine yard line –

SHANA. *(off)* Peruvians give you hiccups.

ETHAN. Oh, yeah.

HAMPTON. WILL YOU JUST LISTEN TO ME FOR ONCE? Everything's fine, all right!?! We're not going to have to move, we're not going to have to do anything except be vampires in the real world. So, there's no reason to move, okay?

ETHAN. Thousands of people now *know* that you guys are vampires, *and* what you look like. And thank you *so much* for mentioning *my* name.

(Enter **SHANA**.*)*

HAMPTON. He asked me who made me a vampire.

ETHAN. I didn't do it! It was Earl! *Evido – fuck!*

HAMPTON. I wasn't *about* to admit to that on TV. Yes, Brady, I was bitten by a guy named "*Earl*". Why, yes, Brady, he *does* wear a cape –

ETHAN. Know what happens now? People knocking on our door bearing torches, holding thermoses full of holy water and a hand full of wooden stakes. Crazies with crucifixes –

HAMPTON. You have to learn to have a little faith in me, brother. Remember that time in '68 – 1968 – when you and I took some LSD, and you didn't want to take it because you were afraid of what might happen? You had the best trip ever. You saw things that you didn't think were possible. You felt as if the world had just opened up to you and was accepting you for what you were. And then, after you came down, you *thanked me.* And all because of a little trust.

ETHAN. That's not what happened. I thought I was a meadowlark, climbed a tree, tried to fly, and broke my collarbone.

HAMPTON. Then who was –

ETHAN. I don't know. But later in the hospital – that's how fucked up we were, that someone thought it would be a good idea to bring me to a hospital.

SHANA. I remember *that.*

HAMPTON. Okay, this is going to bug me, who –

ETHAN. It doesn't matter!

HAMPTON. Back me up here, Daniel.

DANIEL. It looks all right to me. I mean, after we went to the zoo, we went to this bar, and this woman came up to me being really nice to me, saying she had seen me on TV, and then she bought me some milk. I don't really like milk, but she was nice.

HAMPTON. You see? Milk! Doesn't that make you think?

ETHAN. *(to SHANA)* How about Madagascar? Should we move there?

SHANA. Only if you want to spend all day eating tarsiers.

ETHAN. What the hell's a tarsier?

HAMPTON. We can't move, this is our power base. Our headquarters. The Batcave.

ETHAN. Oh, yes, we're going to have to move. And do you know where we're going to have to move to? Greenland. And I *hate* Greenland! It's cold in Greenland! We'll have to eat penguins!

HAMPTON. They don't have penguins in Greenland.

EARL. I am leaving. Good night.

ETHAN. You can't leave, I told you.

EARL. Your childish banter bores me. I do not care to be privy to it any longer. I hunger.

ETHAN. Fine. But stay close.

EARL. *(beat)* Be careful of that which you seek, Hampton. You do not look ahead to the consequences.

HAMPTON. Was that a threat?

EARL. You are not alone in this world.

(**EARL** *exits through front door.*)

HAMPTON. That sound like a threat to you?

ETHAN. No, but this might…You do anything like this again…if this doesn't blow over and soon…then you and me…wow, can't tell you how bad it will be.

HAMPTON. Does that mean I should cancel the reporter who's coming over here tomorrow night?

ETHAN. Ha, ha, ha.

(**ETHAN** *exits to hallway.*)

SHANA. *(beat)* You just like getting on his nerves.

HAMPTON. There's no challenge anymore.

SHANA. Your hair's a mess, Daniel. What did you do at the zoo?

(SHANA *starts detangling* DANIEL*'s hair.*)

DANIEL. I just watched the monkeys.

HAMPTON. He climbed a tree in Monkey World.

SHANA. Hold still.

HAMPTON. So you wanna get in on this deal, Shana? I figure if you join up, Ethan might be a little more comfy with the situation, you know?

SHANA. I could give a damn about your big plans.

HAMPTON. We'll see how you feel once this thing starts to pick up steam. Just wait 'til the book comes out. I've already talked to a publisher. We're in negotiations.

SHANA. I'm going to do you a favor and not tell Ethan about this. Mainly because I don't think you'll go through with it.

HAMPTON. He's talking advance –

SHANA. *(to* DANIEL*)* Stop squirming.

DANIEL. I don't feel tangled anymore.

SHANA. Well, you are.

DANIEL. But I don't *feel* tangled.

HAMPTON. That means *money*.

SHANA. You need a shower. I'll go start you one.

DANIEL. No, wait! I don't mind this really. It's sorta like when monkeys groom each other.

HAMPTON. Will you shut up about the monkeys already!?!

SHANA. Don't snap at him!

(SHANA *smacks* HAMPTON *across the head and exits to hallway.*)

HAMPTON. Okay, okay! Geez. *(pause)* Sorry I snapped at you, Daniel.

DANIEL. It'd be nice if you wouldn't yell at me so much.

HAMPTON. You're right. I shouldn't do that. So, here's what we do. If you back me on this move, I'll try to control my temper. Because we're *family*. And family sticks together, am I right? Right. Now why don't you go round us up some desert for tonight? Try to find us an Italian, okay?

DANIEL. I like Italians. Much more than milk.

HAMPTON. Well, then, go grab us some, why don't ya, tiger?

*(**DANIEL** opens his coffin and pulls out a large sack. He runs out the front door just as **SHANA** enters.)*

SHANA. Daniel! Where's he going?

HAMPTON. Food run.

SHANA. Why am I running a shower then?

*(**SHANA** exits to hallway.)*

HAMPTON. Italian – you in? *(A moment. **HAMPTON** speaks into his tape recorder.)* I feel...like I'm leading a bunch of blind people around. All they can see is the bad. What about the good? I'm just trying to show them that the good is...good, and if I can make all this good, then isn't that...good? *(pause)* I'll just edit this part. Anyway...Daniel. He gets it, even if he is a little slow. I shouldn't say that.

*(**ETHAN** enters.)*

He's a sweet kid. The rest will get it, too. Well, maybe not Earl, but...

ETHAN. Asshole.

*(**HAMPTON** turns off his recorder.)*

HAMPTON. Jealous much?

*(Exit **HAMPTON**, passing **SHANA**. **ETHAN** collapses in his recliner.)*

SHANA. You okay?

ETHAN. I've lived for a long time in secrecy...going about my business...only to see the one thing that could end us entirely. Publicity. I mean, before it was easy. Someone found dead with teeth marks on their neck? Wild animal. Tragic.

SHANA. You're over-thinking again.

(*Enter* **EARL** *from kitchen.*)

HAMPTON. *(off)* WHO HAS BEEN USING MY COLOGNE?

ETHAN. NO ONE USES THAT COLOGNE EXCEPT YOU!

SHANA. Calm down. *(beat)* Did you bring us back something, Evido?

EARL. I have left the remains in the kitchen.

SHANA. Want anything, dear?

ETHAN. Not hungry.

(**SHANA** *exits to kitchen.*)

EARL. Hampton and Daniel are becoming hazardous.

ETHAN. As far as dealing with this, I'm open to suggestions. *(beat)* Aw, hell, let's just kill him.

EARL. No. That is an unforgivable act.

ETHAN. I was kidding – take it easy. The way Hampton's going, he'll end up killing himself.

EARL. And Daniel with him.

Scene Seven

(Spotlight on the **HUNTER***.)*

HUNTER. I was eight. In bed, not able to sleep. Havin' a thirst, so I wanted a glass of water. Careful not to disturb my folks, case they was sleepin' or doin' stuff that eight year old's ought not to see. *(beat)* Thought I saw somethin'. The guy on top of my mama wasn't my daddy. Had long black hair like a girl's. Daddy musta been at the bar is what I thought. Took matters into my own hands. Grabbed the bee-bee rifle I got for Christmas. Took aim and shot the sumbitch in the ass. He was payin' attention now. Had blood all over his face. Mama open wide – eyes, mouth, nose, all of it open and torn to death. Saw my daddy's body on the carpet, blood sucked clean, hands and feet curled up. I figgered the bloody sumbitch was waitin' for me to cry or scream or somethin'. *(beat)* Just stood there, holding my bee-bee rifle…He walks up to me, I'm aimin' at his head. He kneels down, the stink of his breath comin' at me. *(beat)* "This is your lucky day, sport. I'm full." *(beat)* First one I *kilt* was working at a Coney Island diner. Splattered his guts all over the stale fries in the dumpster. *(beat)* They're everywhere, you know? Look like you and me. That's why they're so good at killin', cuz you don't know, really know, who's a vampire, and who ain't.

(He pulls out a bright green pamphlet and shows it to the audience.)

HUNTER. Got a problem? Find one-a-these. Call the number.

Scene Eight

(Light change. The next night. **ETHAN** *is reading his book. Enter* **HAMPTON.***)*

HAMPTON. Where's Earl? He's gonna miss all the action.

ETHAN. One of these days, Evido's going to just haul off and smack you, you know? What action?

HAMPTON. Are you hanging out tonight?

ETHAN. Might as well. Slim pickin's out there right now. Guess whose fault that is.

HAMPTON. Give it time.

ETHAN. I give it a week. It'll blow over. No one watches Brady Lennox anyway except drunks and students... who are also drunk.

HAMPTON. That's the spirit.

ETHAN. Where's Danny?

HAMPTON. Food run. I was thinking Arabic tonight, so –

ETHAN. Another food run? Do you hunt at *all* anymore, you lazy bastard?

HAMPTON. I had shit to do.

ETHAN. Do tell.

HAMPTON. I don't see *Shana* around anywhere.

SHANA. *(off)* Shana's in the kitchen! Also thinking you're a lazy bastard!

HAMPTON. If you all are just going to gang up on me like this, then no Arab for you.

(a knock at front door)

ETHAN. Tell the late night Jesus freaks to go away.

HAMPTON. Take it easy. Danny probably just forgot his key.

ETHAN. *(stands up)* What's that smell?

*(***HAMPTON*** opens the door for* **CHRISTY** *and* **CAM-ERAMAN** *to enter.* **ETHAN** *immediately dashes into the kitchen.)*

HAMPTON. Christy, babe! Good to see you. Are we ready to do this?

CHRISTY. I am, are you?

HAMPTON. Should we sit?

CHRISTY. Sure, sure, just be as comfortable as possible. Oh, and let's get this on you.

(The CAMERAMAN clips a transmitter to HAMPTON.)

HAMPTON. I'm a little nervous, I gotta tell you.

CHRISTY. Just relax and be yourself. Think of our viewing audience as a big group of friends. Or better yet, one really good friend. No, better yet, ignore them, just talk to me, kay? Super.

(The CAMERAMAN picks up his camera and aims it at HAMPTON.)

HAMPTON. Is this going out live?

CHRISTY. Is that okay?

HAMPTON. It's fine. Let's do this.

CAMERAMAN. And in 5, 4, 3…(motion two, one, go.)

CHRISTY. This is Christy Banks for Fox News, coming to you live from an undisclosed location where myth has recently become exposed as fact. If you were up late last night and happened to be watching local TV program The Brady Lennox Show, you may have seen something like this…

(a moment)

HAMPTON. What's – ?

CHRISTY. We're inserting a clip here. (returning) A parlor trick? A circus act? CGI? Vampires have been a part of our culture for decades, but always under the assumption that they were the stuff of children's nightmares or big budget Hollywood movies, or, to a lesser extent, literature. But just last night on The Brady Lennox Show, this man, known only as Hampton, showed local residents the reality of true-to-life vampirism, by sucking the blood out of a sheep in just under one minute.

Ladies and gentlemen, I give you Hampton, the *vampire. (beat)* Congratulations to you, Hampton, for having the courage to "come out of the coffin", as it were.

HAMPTON. *(chuckling politely)* "Coming out of the...", that's very –

CHRISTY. Why now? Why in this day and age have you chosen to reveal yourself?

HAMPTON. Well, Christy, I probably would have come out during the sixties when people were more open to things, but that whole Vietnam thing, along with the Charles Manson incident...So, why not, Christy? Now why not? Why not *now?*

CHRISTY. Fascinating. Where do you go from here?

HAMPTON. Well, I have been talking to some "people," and we think that the next move would be to establish a sort of legitimacy, first here in the United States, a place I've called home for the last...several years, and then to the rest of the world.

CHRISTY. So, there are others like you in the world, yes?

HAMPTON. I can't hold myself accountable for every mysterious disappearance over the last three centuries. *(they share a laugh)* But seriously...I would really like to see the day come where more of my kind are able to hold their heads up high in public and say once and for all, "yes, I am a vampire." No shame, no guilt, no...shame.

CHRISTY. I guess the question on everyone's mind is does this new revelation mean that vampires would give up killing human beings for food? Some would think you nothing more than a monster. A monster who *murders.*

HAMPTON. I don't think of it as murder, Christy. I think of it as a means of survival, which I'm sure, anyone could relate to.

CHRISTY. Who do you eat that *deserves* to die? Who is on your list as edible, Hampton? Old people? Retarded children? *Winos?*

HAMPTON. Human beings are just going to have to accept that they are no longer the top link in the food chain. I mean, I *totally* understand the situation, believe me. I mean, I wouldn't want anyone to eat *me*, obviously.

CHRISTY. Well, I'm sure our viewing audience would like to know why you should be given special privilege. Why *you* should be allowed to murder.

(Enter **DANIEL** *through front door. He is carrying a sack with a tennis-shoed leg sticking out of it.)*

HAMPTON. Oh, good. Here's my friend Daniel – also a vampire – come on in, Danny.

*(***HAMPTON*** anxiously signals* **DANIEL** *to put the bag down and out of view.)*

CHRISTY. Hello, Daniel. Are you a vampire as well?

DANIEL. Yes.

HAMPTON. Danny was the first to…"come out of the coffin" with me.

CHRISTY. Fascinating. Now, what about this murdering business?

HAMPTON. I eat, I live, Christy. If you were in my position, you would think the same way.

CHRISTY. Any parting words, Hampton?

HAMPTON. *(thinks)* Don't judge us, America. We're much more than a pain in the neck.

CHRISTY. *(to camera)* Hampton. He's a vampire, and proud of it. This is Christy Banks for Fox News, thanking you, and thanking Hampton the vampire. Stay tuned for *Money Matters*.

CAMERAMAN. And we're clear.

CHRISTY. *(to* **CAMERAMAN**.*)* Let's go. Don't leave without me, now. *(beat)* Hampton. Thank you for this opportunity. Maybe we can do a follow-up in a few weeks, just to see how you're doing? Possibly talk about a hour long expose?

HAMPTON. Sure, sure. You have my number. Get a hold of me. We'll talk.

CHRISTY. Super. Thank you again.

(CHRISTY *exits.*)

CAMERAMAN. So, what makes you think people will jump on this bandwagon with you? I mean, you guys are technically the bad guys, am I right?

HAMPTON. *(beat)* I know that camera guys such as yourself often find themselves in compromising situations…so, I guess, I would like to know…at what *point* does the decision to flee come up?

CAMERAMAN. Hey, I'm on the clock.

(CAMERAMAN *exits.*)

HAMPTON. *(to Danny)* That went well, don't you think?

(Enter EARL *and* SHANA *from kitchen.*)

DANIEL. Are we gonna be on TV again?

SHANA. "We're much more than a pain in the neck?" You're such a moron.

HAMPTON. It's called schmoozing. And schmoozing is not something to be taken lightly if you're going to get ahead in the world, babe.

SHANA. Go suck someone's ass, Hampton.

HAMPTON. See? That's not schmoozing.

EARL. You are a disgrace to our order.

HAMPTON. Oh, I do NOT want to hear it from *you*, Earl! It's not an *order!* It's just the five of us!

EARL. You make us meat for the lessers.

HAMPTON. Bite me.

EARL. If only I could.

DANIEL. I brought home Arabic! It's still warm!

ETHAN. *(off)* Hey, is Hampton out there?

HAMPTON. Yeah, Ethan, I'm here.

ETHAN. Good. Because I'm going to FUCKING KILL YOU!

(ETHAN *runs out and slams* HAMPTON *into the ground.*)

ETHAN. SOMEBODY GRAB ME A PIECE OF THE KITCHEN TABLE SO I CAN RAM THIS BASTARD THROUGH HIS STERNUM!

(**DANIEL** *and* **SHANA** *pull* **ETHAN** *off.*)

SHANA. THAT'S ENOUGH!

ETHAN. You've fucked us, Hampton! What were you thinking!?! That smiling pretty for the camera with those flesh-tearing fangs of yours would make people *love us!?!*

HAMPTON. Not right away –

ETHAN. I can't take this! I can't take you, Hampton! I can't watch you kill us!

HAMPTON. United we stand –

ETHAN. Extinction! Is that a word you know!?! *(beat)* Learn it.

(**ETHAN** *heads for the door.*)

SHANA. Where are you going?

ETHAN. Out.

SHANA. When will you be back?

(**ETHAN** *exits.*)

HAMPTON. Yeah, that's right! You go away now! And when this thing gets a full head of steam, you just SEE IF YOUR NAME'S ON OUR MAILING LIST! *(into recorder)* It's just this kind of thinking that makes my kind of thinking so difficult! *(exiting to hallway)* CHAPTER SEVEN! STUBBORN JACKASSES!

(**SHANA** *reacts to the noise and sits on the coffin, holding her head.*)

SHANA. Remember a time when it wasn't so freakin' loud all the time?

EARL. That was a very long time ago.

SHANA. Was it? Do tell.

EARL. *(pause)* Quiet save for the gentle lapping of the wind on the trees. A saddened girl sat at the edge of a lonely grave marked only with a cross made of sticks.

SHANA. Hey, now. I wasn't asking for –

EARL. She wept.

SHANA. Yeah. *(beat)* Fuckin' hell, Evido.

DANIEL. That was you.

EARL. At first you were sustenance. Another call to blood… but then…

DANIEL. I thought you looked nice. You seemed so sad, but you looked nice, and I thought that we could be friends and that we could make you happy. So I bit you.

EARL. And so it was. The world grew louder after you.

SHANA. *(chuckling)* Not my fault. Don't go blaming me for…*(pause)* That was my mother's grave. She was… they – the community got it into their heads that she was a witch. So they…torches and…they took her… They made this little cross out of sticks and rope and stuck it in the ground and asked God to forgive her. It obviously wasn't their job, was it? Sure as shit not even a grave anymore – probably a strip mall over it or something – why am I even talking? – I mean, this was like a hundred years after Salem – get over it already, you know? *(beat)* Man, that's the last of the quiet you remember? Because that was a loud day for me. Thanks for bringing *that* up. Geez.

DANIEL. *(beat)* We're never going to leave.

(a moment)

SHANA. *(kissing* DANIEL *on the head)* Sometimes I really love you guys.

*(*SHANA *gives* EARL *a peck on the cheek the exits to bedroom area. A moment.)*

EARL. That was…pleasant.

DANIEL. Yeah. *(beat)* Do you like monkeys, Lord Evido?

EARL. I am indifferent toward monkeys.

DANIEL. Oh. But, you know what I like about them? They're very family-oriented. *(beat)* Do you ever have trouble sleeping because of bad dreams, Lord Evido?

EARL. I do not.

DANIEL. Oh. *(beat)* I think I'll take a nap. I'm really tired.

(DANIEL opens his coffin.)

EARL. Sleep well, my brother.

DANIEL. Don't let me sleep too long, okay? My favorite show on the nature channel will be on later. They're doing a show on lemurs. I don't wanna miss it.

EARL. As you wish.

(DANIEL closes the coffin lid. Enter HAMPTON speaking into recorder.)

HAMPTON. What am I doing wrong? *(beat)* NOTHING! I'm just trying to make our lives easier, and I can't do that if PEOPLE KEEP YELLING AT ME! *(beat)* A chance to step up in the world! We're an advance in the evolutionary process, and we're just…just supposed to hide!?! Well, we'll just see. I'm going to give vampires peace of mind even if they don't think they really want it! THEN WE CAN ALL BE HAPPY, GODDAMMIT! *(pause, to EARL)* WHAT!?!

(blackout)

ACT II

Scene Nine

(Two months later. Spotlight on **CHRISTY BANKS**.*)*

CHRISTY. Vampires. Evil spawns spat from the mouth of Hell, or new cultural good guys? One can never tell about these things until you sit down and have a conversation with one of them and realize that they are nearly as human as you and I, they just live longer. In the last two months, I've interviewed many vampires besides Hampton, and what impressed me the most is that they never once tried to eat me.

*(***EARL*** lurks in the background.)*

Oh, sure they could have, and there are many, many victims out there, and I think that says a lot. In fact, I would suggest becoming buddy-buddy with a vampire. If they know who you are, they will be less likely to eat you. Talk to them cordially, never *ever* talk down to them, treat them as you would your closest friend. They'll appreciate it. And they won't eat you. *(seeing* **EARL***)* Hello? Oh, hello! Power to the people, Mr. Vampire!

*(***EARL*** quickly consumes* **CHRISTY**. **CHRISTY** *screams.)*

Scene Ten

(HAMPTON, GRETCHEN, LUCINA, TRESA, *and* DANIEL *lounge around with bottles of blood and note-books.*)

GRETCHEN. They want us to accept a law that would prohibit any known vampire from holding an elected office.

TRESA. There have been vampires in office before.

GRETCHEN. I said *known* vampires. No one knows about Alexander Hamilton. Or Andrew Jackson. Or Spiro Agnew.

TRESA. How is Spiro? Is he still living in Brazil?

HAMPTON. It's all about give and take.

GRETCHEN. They're also bringing up the idea of us resorting to blood banks.

HAMPTON. Next they'll offer us cows.

GRETCHEN. No cows. They need those for food. They were thinking more along the lines of dogs and cats scheduled for termination.

LUCINA. They would *never* say that if they knew what dog blood tasted like.

HAMPTON. I'll tell you what, in darker days, when I had to resort to eating animals for weeks, I felt like Hell.

GRETCHEN. You should write that down. Put it in your book.

HAMPTON. Think I will. *(beat)* What did I just…? *(beat)* This is *exactly* why we need to hire a stenographer.

GRETCHEN. Thought that was what the recorder was for.

(*Enter* SHANA *through front door.*)

SHANA. Are we fighting the good fight?

HAMPTON. Care to join us, sister Shana?

SHANA. Let me mull it over – No.

HAMPTON. Things are happening. Balls are rolling. There's no reason that we can't –

SHANA. Do you know how hungry I am? Nightlife is scarce out there right now –

GRETCHEN. If you're not with us, you're against us. As a spokesperson –

SHANA. YOU DON'T SPEAK FOR ALL OF US! *(composing)* As long as I am considered a nightmare, I plan to stay that way. So you, and your little group? You can all go bite yourselves.

GRETCHEN. Solidarity, Shana.

SHANA. Suck ass, Gretchen.

GRETCHEN. It's vampires like you that make it hard for the rest of us to gain acceptance.

SHANA. And it's vampires like *you* that make it hard for the rest of us to *live.*

(**SHANA** *pulls a pamphlet out of her pocket. She slams it down on the coffin.*)

SHANA. Know what this is? It's a pamphlet. Guess what it's offering. "Vampire problem? Exterminate. Immediately. Call soon, before it's too late." These are decorating telephone poles all over. Is this the kind of publicity you were looking for?

HAMPTON. You're beginning to sound like Ethan.

(**SHANA** *shoots* **HAMPTON** *a hard glance, then exits.*)

GRETCHEN. *(beat)* Would we consent to allow vampires to not live past the age of one-hundred and fifty years?

LUCINA. They're asking for the world. Over and over again, they want to keep themselves free and clear from being ordinary. Cows don't ask why they need to be made into hamburgers. Sheep don't ask why you have to shave them down to make sweaters. Vegetarians don't consider carrots as living things when they eat them. Cows moo, humans cry out to God, and carrots don't scream. *Whoopee.* Who gives a rat's ass? It's all food in the end.

TRESA. Okay, stay with me on this one. When they ask us who we should feed on...tell them that we will agree to eat *only* the homeless. I mean, they're always complaining about the homeless population, right? So, we can, one, feed ourselves, and two, perform a community service.

GRETCHEN. And when we're done with the homeless?

TRESA. We move up to the lower middle class, I suppose.

HAMPTON. It implies elimination. We're trying to avoid that argument. In ten years, we would pretty much do away with the homeless problem, provided we were all hungry enough to eat things that dirty, and then what? Focus on the working man? We'd have the unions on our backs. There has to be a sense of equal distribution.

GRETCHEN. Are we going to become *socialist* vampires, Hampton?

HAMPTON. Socialism? Not likely. *(into recorder)* This is pure Democracy. A system in which everyone regardless of sex, race, or class, has the chance of being eaten.

*(Knock. **DANIEL** goes for the front door.)*

It's not a bad concept. We can dress it up.

*(**DANIEL** opens the door to see a man with an envelope.)*

MAN. Mr. Hampton?

HAMPTON. *(walking to door)* Yes?

*(The man hands **HAMPTON** the envelope and leaves. **HAMPTON** opens it up and reads the letter inside.)*

Oh, man.

LUCINA. What?

HAMPTON. Oh, MAN! She told me she was eighteen! She *looked* eighteen!

GRETCHEN. What is it!?!

HAMPTON. I'm being sued!

GRETCHEN. Are you kidding me?

HAMPTON. This girl I met at a bar...a couple of months ago...she wanted to become a vampire so I...helped her out. But guess what? She's a minor, and her parents are suing me!

LUCINA. *(grabbing summons)* Can they do that? What's the charge?

HAMPTON. *(grabbing summons)* Contributing to the delinquency of a minor and...statutory rape!?!

GRETCHEN. *(grabbing summons)* Are you kidding? How is this statutory rape?

HAMPTON. *(grabbing summons)* Because they don't have a law for statutory vampirism yet.

LUCINA. *(grabbing summons)* Shouldn't Hampton be arrested for it, then?

HAMPTON. *(grabbing summons)* This is a civil suit.

LUCINA. *(grabbing summons)* Am I supposed to know the difference?

HAMPTON. *(grabbing summons)* Only when it happens to *you.*

(HAMPTON *holds the summons high, out of reach of* GRETCHEN.*)*

GRETCHEN. They can't get away with this. It looks like just another publicity stunt or get rich quick scheme. But more than that...it looks *really bad* for us. Can I see that, please?

HAMPTON. Bad for us? Excuse *me?* It's my cute little ass on the line here, babe!

LUCINA. *(grabbing summons)* What happens to one of us happens to all of us.

HAMPTON. Then you'll help me pay the settlement?

LUCINA. *(giving summons back) No,* but...how much was your advance for the book?

HAMPTON. All gone! Remember? Stamps? Envelopes? Flyers? Late night publicity luncheons? LARGE DONATIONS TO CANCER KID ORGANIZATIONS, PROMISING THAT WE WOULDN'T EAT THEM *BECAUSE* THEY HAD CANCER!?! With the advance, and all the commercials, and the cameos...we *should* have *some* money, don't you think?

GRETCHEN. PR costs money, Hampton.

HAMPTON. So do lawsuits, Gretchen!

TRESA. Do we know any vampires that are lawyers? Maybe do a pro bono kind of thing?

GRETCHEN. Oddly enough, no. That doesn't mean they don't exist – we'll make some calls.

TRESA. Publish the book! Just write something out! It doesn't even have to be good! With the hype behind it, we'll be able to cover the court costs by the first week sales alone!

GRETCHEN. Perfect! Just finish the book, Hampton! Or… *start it*, at least! You didn't know she was a minor. She lied to you. Was it in a bar? IT WAS THE BAR'S FAULT FOR NOT PROPERLY CHECKING HER ID! WE'LL SUE THE BAR! We'll sue the bar and pay for the court costs with the winnings! God, I'm starving! Let's discuss this over lunch!

(The girls chatter away, dragging **DANIEL** *along through the front door.* **HAMPTON** *speaks to his recorder, during which* **EARL** *enters.)*

HAMPTON. Being a celebrity has its upsides. For example… I get to write this book. On the downside? *(beat)* I get to write this book. And deal with deadlines and…food isn't so easy to come by anymore. If people catch sight of me coming, they either scream and run away or… they ask for an autograph. And sometimes I oblige them…other times…well, ya gotta eat, right? *(beat)* Note to myself: be choosy about an editor. And…take another trip to the massage parlor.

*(***HAMPTON** *turns off the recorder. He senses* **EARL** *and turns around.)*

Hello, *Lord Evido.* How long have you been here?

EARL. You make a mockery out of what we are. You and your little friends.

HAMPTON. Are we having a heart to heart?

EARL. We were never meant to be understood. We hang in the shadows, make food of the lessers, and survive through the ages. You take away what gives us life.

The veil. The disguise. That which allows us to exist in peace. And after the veil is removed...so goes the hunt.

HAMPTON. *(beat)* You know what? This whole...with the cape and the sour demeanor...it's *old*. The rest of us? We keep with the times, we adapt, but *you*...you're still stuck in the old world.

EARL. And your life is...?

HAMPTON. There is *nothing* wrong with *my life!* Except the fact that I have been hanging around the same four people for so long that – what am I? Nothing unless I'm around you guys, right? Because you guys verify me being a part of the world, right? WRONG! You guys only keep me *outside* of the world! Before this, I was something in the world. I was real.

EARL. Was this life not enough to satisfy your reality?

HAMPTON. The novelty wears off after a while. Before I was alive. It made a difference to people. Because someday I would die after a short amount of time, and that made me real. Now, I live and I live...and I live and I live and I live! And I watch humans and cultures and centuries die, and here I am...and to not even be able to talk about it? To have this part of me, this *important* part of me – have it be my little secret? People know me now. They recognize my face, they ask for autographs, they watch me on TV. They *acknowledge* my *existence.*

EARL. *(beat)* In this we only see that you have exchanged one myth for another.

HAMPTON. *(pause)* You ate Christy banks, didn't you?

EARL. I do not know the names of humans you refer to, nor do I care to.

HAMPTON. Okay, see, I know this means nothing to you, but *me?* I have to deal with it. Do you know what the girls are telling me now? I should pick up and head off like Ethan did.

(Hampton's cell phone rings. **HAMPTON** *debates, then answers.)*

HAMPTON. *(cont.)* Hello? What? Excuse me!?! OH, YEAH!?! WELL, WHY DON'T YOU COME ON OUT AND TALK BIG LIKE YOU DO, SO I CAN EAT YOUR FACE OFF!?!

(**HAMPTON** *hangs up. He turns on the recorder.* **SHANA** *enters.*)

(to recorder) Who are these people who take time out of their days just to call people up and threaten them or tell them how much they hate them or I don't know what! There has to be better ways of occupying their short little lives! Doesn't anybody *bowl* anymore!?!

(**HAMPTON** *turns off the recorder and looks at* **SHANA.**)

I'm fine. I'm *fine.* How are you? It was just a prank call. That's all. Nothing to concern ourselves with. Just a prank call. WHY DOES THIS HAVE TO BE SO GODDAMN HARD!?! I'm fine. Fine. Woo! Look at me be fine! I am fine all over the place fine. The end will justify the means. The girls need me to see this through.

SHANA. Don't do it for them. Forget I said that…don't *do it.*

HAMPTON. I'm taking care of it.

SHANA. But who's going to take care of *you?* I don't like worrying about you this much.

HAMPTON. Yeah. I'm not used to this. You being the worrywart. Knock it off, would ya?

SHANA. Okay. *(beat) Jackass.*

HAMPTON. Thanks, babe. Love ya.

(**HAMPTON***'s phone rings.*)

Maybe it's Ethan.

SHANA. It's not.

(**SHANA** *exits to kitchen.* **HAMPTON** *mutters and answers the phone.*)

HAMPTON. Hello? *Hellooooo?* I know you're there, I can smell you.

(DANIEL enters through the front door.)

THE LEAST YOU COULD DO IS THREATEN TO BURN DOWN MY HOUSE OR KILL MY DOG OR SOMETHING!

(HAMPTON hangs up.)

DANIEL. Did we get a dog?

HAMPTON. *(beat)* I'm going to take a shower. Hold my calls!

(HAMPTON exits to bedroom area.)

DANIEL. So, we *don't* have a dog?

EARL. Hampton is a bad influence on you. Why do you follow him?

DANIEL. He's my friend.

EARL. He treats you like a subordinate. Not like one of his own.

DANIEL. But he takes me places. Like the zoo.

EARL. Ask yourself why he does not treat you like his brother.

DANIEL. Like the zoo, and bowling alleys, and clothing stores, and to the zoo.

EARL. He cares more for those intrusive females. What is this hold Hampton possesses over you?

DANIEL. He talks to me! He *listens* to me! And now, I get to talk to lots of different people and they listen to me and that's because of Hampton! *(beat)* I mean, I know you guys think I'm stupid, and sometimes I say stupid things, but...but I'm just like you guys, right?

(A moment. EARL touches DANIEL's shoulder. He spots the pamphlet.)

EARL. Yes, you are one of us. And I am sorry.

DANIEL. It's okay. It just bothers me sometimes, you know?

EARL. Yes. I do.

DANIEL. I didn't mean to yell.

(SHANA enters from kitchen. EARL recoils his hand from DANIEL.)

SHANA. Don't let me interrupt.

DANIEL. We were just talking.

SHANA. We have *nothing* that looks good to me in the fridge. So, how about me and my two favorite guys go out and grab us something to eat?

EARL. Very well. But...

SHANA. *(beat)* What?

EARL. *(beat)* Let us go.

(SHANA *and* DANIEL *head for the front door. As they speak,* EARL *picks up the pamphlet and exits to hallway.)*

SHANA. Dibs on any Asians.

DANIEL. You *always* call Asians.

SHANA. And *you* always call Indian.

DANIEL. Well, what if I want Asian?

SHANA. Then maybe I'll share.

(SHANA *notices* EARL *is gone.)*

SHANA. Huh. He can be so flaky sometimes.

(DANIEL *tries to exit the front door, but* SHANA *catches his arm.)*

Know what? Let's go through the back door. Just to be safe.

(SHANA *and* DANIEL *exit through kitchen. A moment. A barrage of knocks at the door.)*

HAMPTON. *(off)* Could somebody get that? Hello? I'm naked here! Is anybody home? Danny? Shana? Earl? *(beat)* Evido? *(beat)* DAMMIT!

(HAMPTON *enters putting on a robe.)*

Who is it? Danny?

VANRUEGEN. *(off)* Mr. Hampton. My name is Special Agent Vanruegen. I would like a few moments of your time.

(HAMPTON *opens the door.)*

HAMPTON. Special Agent, huh? What department?

(VANRUEGEN *enters flashing his ID.)*

VANRUEGEN. The Department of Secret Shit – do you want to hear what I have to say or what?

HAMPTON. Come in.

VANRUEGEN. Nice place. Good decor. The All-American home. I like that. Modern, but not without a sense of antiquity. You like living here? Comfort is important, you know what I mean?

HAMPTON. Are you here to talk to me about my home, or my income, or – because I *pay* my taxes.

VANRUEGEN. What am I? The IRS? What do I care if you pay your taxes or not? If you didn't pay your taxes, then it would be someone else visiting you and not me, am I right?

HAMPTON. I have no idea.

(**VANRUEGEN** *lights a cigarette.*)

VANRUEGEN. But for the record? It's *good* that you pay your taxes. Mind if I smoke? So, what is it then? I'm getting a Germanic vibe off you.

HAMPTON. Irish.

VANRUEGEN. Straight Irish? You lost the accent.

HAMPTON. Are you from Immigration?

VANRUEGEN. Of course not. Tossing Mexicans back across the border? Who wants that job?

HAMPTON. Right. Can I ask –

VANRUEGEN. Look, I'll talk to the talk and get right to the point, all right? You are a vampire. But you're not just any ol' vampire. Right now, you are *King Shit* Vampire, and you're out there, talking to the masses, leading this here movement to gain minority status for you and your kind. Hell, I saw you just last night making the circuit, talking the cause, sinking your teeth into the pounding public heart. I watch you giving your interviews and I think, "now, *there's* a vampire with something to say." You are the most fascinating, dangerous thing out there, and everybody knows it. Hell, you don't even *need* a political movement to pull this off. You could just be a celebrity. But you wanted a bit more, didn't you? And that's fine. You can do that. Others have. Women, blacks, homosexuals…hell, even *pedophiles* wanted rights with that whole NAMBLA thing, which is all but buried at this point. And all these groups went through some major-league traumatizations to get as far as they have, which isn't that far in the big picture when you look at it, am I right? Of course, you have the advantage, because you could *actually* live long enough to see progress happen. Human beings and vampires holding hands, smiling happy smiles for each other, not giving a good god damn about who's next to be eaten. A world in which creatures capable of rational thought line up to become a meal for the new world order. In fact, why not just take over the world? Because obviously the world wasn't meant exclusively for humans to rule, am I right? And that means God screwed up. And God doesn't make mistakes, does he? Maybe he meant for vampires to happen, and you can take pride in that, if there is a God, and I'm not saying there is, but wouldn't it be nice to think that *finally* there was an evolutionary path for *mosquitoes* to follow? We can't seem to find a great idea as to why those little maggots exist, but maybe the answer is vampires. And if it is the work of Darwinism or Godism or any other ism you care to throw out there, then why not? And that's what you're working for, isn't it?

HAMPTON. Can you just tell me what this is all about?

VANRUEGEN. I'll be straight with you. The United States Government is uncomfortable with this movement. Makes them feel like all these years of feeling superior are falling away from them, and they're scrambling around, as politicians will do, wondering what they can do to control the uncontrollable. Should we kill them off? Maybe. But how would that look? To take a pro-extinction stance? Call them terrorists, and eliminate them like that? No can do. Because you're media-friendly, especially that Danny kid you sometimes drag along with you. Oh, people *like* him, let me tell you. Even more than you. And they wouldn't want to see anything bad happen to him. So, here's what we do. We settle things here and now. You want to become a part of this country? How do we do this? Without movements? Without protests? Without the clamor and clang of upset religious groups insisting you're just another piece of the Devil? Well, I'll tell you. We are very interested in starting up a very secretive division, within the call of the National Security – maybe the CIA, FBI, that's to be decided at a later date – where you vampires can infiltrate unfriendlies, because you all seem to have a knack for slipping past securities and whatnot, and setting yourselves up in cozy situations without anyone being the wiser. Once in, you feed us information, or you kill who we tell you to. Given permission by the most powerful government in the world to feed on the tyrannical forces that are constantly waiting for us to slip. You get to eat the bad guys, and let me tell you, that's a pretty long menu, if you ask me. You got appetizers, soups of the day, chef's specials, four fucking entrees waiting for you. Hell of a deal, if you ask me.

HAMPTON. Not such a secret, is it, since everyone in the world who owns a TV or reads a paper knows that we exist.

VANRUEGEN. It would take no time at all of the media's ignoring of it to wipe it out completely. In two months, I guarantee, the only vampire issues brought up will be at bars among drunk-fucks who can't help but talk. No hassle, no bullshit, no half-assed explanations. So, what do you say, vampire guy? Are we fighting the good fight or what?

HAMPTON. And the alternative is?

VANRUEGEN. Do you want to *hear* the alternative? Fine. The alternative being extreme discomfort. Are we talkin' here or what?

HAMPTON. *(pause, realizing)* You were the cameraman for the first Christy Banks interview weren't you? *(beat)* You were the guy giving out free cheese samples at the supermarket when I went to buy shampoo! *(beat)* You gave me the summons! You were the bartender at Guido's! *(beat)* YOU GAVE ME A MASSAGE! *(beat)* You've been watching me this whole time, haven't you? Well, I got nothing to say to you.

VANRUEGEN. *(beat)* You think long and hard about what I just said, Count Chocula. You can keep trying to promote this equality shtick until the cows come home, but in the end, that will get you zippity-doo-nothing. My way? You serve your country, live the life of feeders, and go back to being the nightmares you once thought was the best thing to ensure your *survival.*

HAMPTON. Please don't make me mad.

VANRUEGEN. Remember what we did to the Japs during World War II? Stuck them in those camps? That's you. Or maybe we'll just exterminate you all one by one, now that we've been taking names. Like shootin' monkeys in a barrel, ain't it? Or better yet, let science be the guiding hand in all this. Can you see it now? You in a sterile room with doctors looking you over, taking samples, possibly learning the secret of making real soldiers into God-fearing vampire protectors of this great nation.

HAMPTON. GET OUT.

VANRUEGEN. WORK FOR US OR GET DEAD! *THOSE* ARE YOUR OPTIONS! IF YOU THINK I'M KIDDIN' AROUND HERE, LOOK IN THE OBITUARY TOMORROW AND SEE WHO YOU KNOW!

(**HAMPTON** *attacks* **VANRUEGEN,** *rushing him offstage. After a moment,* **HAMPTON** *staggers back on, spitting blood, horribly sickened by it.* **VANRUEGEN** *enters holding his neck.)*

VANRUEGEN. OW! *(beat)* You're just a big stupid guy, aren't ya? Your head's too full of public distraction to tell the difference anymore, ain't it? You should know better than to bite one of your own. Leaves a bad taste in your mouth. We'll talk. Real soon. Cuz if we don't... then something's happening, and you can bank on that one. *(beat)* See you around, meatball.

*(**VANRUEGEN** exits. A moment.)*

HAMPTON. GODDAMN GOVERNMENT VAMPIRES!

*(Enter **EARL. HAMPTON** is startled.)*

HAMPTON. Jesus *Christ*, Earl. Can't you make even a *little* noise when you enter a room?

EARL. Who was that man?

HAMPTON. Oh, him? Old college buddy.

EARL. *(beat)* You fear him.

HAMPTON. Hey, fuck you, I do not! I'm not afraid of anything.

EARL. *(beat)* Except death. *(beat)* Was he death?

HAMPTON. *(pause)* Yes.

*(Enter **SHANA** and **DANIEL** through front door.)*

SHANA. *(to EARL)* There you are. Where'd you run off to?

HAMPTON. *(distracted)* HE GAVE ME A MASSAGE!

SHANA. *Evido* gave you a massage? You never give *me* a massage, Evido.

HAMPTON. Can't you see what's happening? Can't any of you? We're...we...if something doesn't happen? Then, submission! Honest to God termination, we're talking here!

EARL. And who will lead us there?

HAMPTON. I need some air! Or food! *Something!*

*(**HAMPTON** exits through the front door.)*

SHANA. Do you think he realizes that he's in his bathrobe?

*(**HAMPTON** re-enters, exits to hallway.)*

Did something happen?

EARL. Death came for a visit.

*(**EARL** exits through front door.)*

SHANA. *(beat)* I hate it when he gets cryptic.

Scene Eleven

(Light change. Enter **VANRUEGEN**, *rubbing his neck. He pulls out his cellphone.)*

VANRUEGEN. Get me Whitt. *(beat)* I don't care if she's in a meeting, get her. *(beat)* Yeah, I'll hold – why wouldn't I hold?

*(***EARL*** *lurks around the opposite side of the stage.* ***VANRUEGEN*** *senses him and hangs up his phone.)*

VANRUEGEN. What are you all got up as, son?

EARL. *(beat)* You betray your own. You have no honor.

VANRUEGEN. *(beat)* You can't be...*(beat)* Dressed like that? *No.* That's just too *cute.*

EARL. You bring shame upon yourself.

VANRUEGEN. And dressing like Christopher Lee doesn't? I am *so* very interested in you.

EARL. You disgrace your kind.

VANRUEGEN. *(beat)* Keep talking. See where it gets you.

EARL. You are *not* one of us.

VANRUEGEN. I am a *survivor*, my friend. Tell me I'm not.

EARL. You are *nothing* to us.

VANRUEGEN. *(beat)* Don't think so? Well...allow me to show you, then.

*(***VANRUEGEN*** *and* ***EARL*** *march toward each other. Just before they collide, blackout.)*

Scene Twelve

(HAMPTON, GRETCHEN, LUCINA, *and* TRESA *in dis-cussion.*)

GRETCHEN. This is what is known as a dilemma.

TRESA. Geez, Hampton. Did you have to try to eat him? He works for the government!

HAMPTON. He pissed me off. He told me that whatever we did wouldn't matter. He said the powers-that-be would never recognize us. *(beat)* Plus, he called me *Count Chocula*, and I *hate that.*

LUCINA. *Jesus*, Hampton, why did you have to go and bite him? Leaders don't bite. *Gandhi* wouldn't have bit him.

GRETCHEN. It's a classic case of oppression. We turn the media on to this and open it up wide.

HAMPTON. That was a *vampire* working for the government, ladies! Doesn't it make you wonder how many more vampires are working for them besides this guy?

TRESA. Well, it would explain a lot.

HAMPTON. This isn't a joke, okay!?! We're talking about full-on *infiltration*, people. They could be everywhere. Waiting for us to slip up. Reporters? Sure. I'd buy that. Barbers, waiters, butchers, actors – hotel clerks? They could be selling us shampoo, pouring our drinks, filling our gas tanks. For the love of God, they could be giving us *massages!* Okay, let's get it all out, is anybody here working for the government? Let's see some hands! Gretchen?

GRETCHEN. Oh, please.

HAMPTON. You're the brains of this outfit, right? You could be setting the bait out for us to take, right? You and your political...stuff.

GRETCHEN. Dammit, Hampton, I haven't voted since Goldwater!

HAMPTON. *(beat)* Okay, never mind. Who cares? We don't have to worry about Vanruegen because vampires don't kill other vampires. Ever. That's just how it is.

They could…hire people to do that, but that's a long time to live with the guilt, am I right? So, let's not worry about this.

(Enter **EARL** *through kitchen.)*

HAMPTON. Hey, Earl. Out and about?

EARL. *(beat)* Death no longer seeks you.

HAMPTON: Excuse me?

EARL. *(beat)* The man you saw as Death. He is no more.

HAMPTON. You… what are you saying? Because it sounds like you're saying –

EARL. I once gave you a gift. Let it be that this thing that I have done, will be the last.

HAMPTON. *(beat)* No. I don't believe you.

*(***EARL*** tosses a filled sack into the room. He exits through the kitchen. ***HAMPTON*** opens the sack.)*

TRESA. What was that all about?

LUCINA. He's so weird.

*(A moment. ***HAMPTON*** shows them the head in the sack.)*

GRETCHEN. Ew. *(beat)* I'm sorry, am I missing the metaphor? Fine. We have work to do, if we're going to fix this situation.

TRESA. Should we do something about the head first?

GRETCHEN. If Earl can't clean up his own messes, then he deserves whatever trouble comes his way.

HAMPTON. We can leave it on the porch. It'll be gone once the sun comes up.

LUCINA. Why? Is it a vampire? *(laughs until she catches* **HAMPTON**'s *look)* Oh, shit.

GRETCHEN. Are you kidding me!?! Oh, something has *got* to be done about this!

HAMPTON. May I introduce the head of Special Agent Vanruegen, ladies?

GRETCHEN. Okay, again, Hampton, I think it may be best to leave Earl and –

(**ETHAN** *enters through the front door with a bag. A moment.*)

HAMPTON. Ethan.

GRETCHEN. *(beat)* Ethan? *This* is *Ethan?* This is fantastic! This is just the kind of happy-homecoming fluff piece that could really help us!

ETHAN. I don't know you three. Get out.

HAMPTON. Hey, could you give us a minute, please?

TRESA. He doesn't have to be rude.

ETHAN. Yes, I do.

HAMPTON. Just go wait in my room and…don't touch my stuff.

(*The girls exit to bedroom area.* **ETHAN** *playfully grabs* **HAMPTON***'s face.*)

ETHAN. Good to see you again, brother.

HAMPTON. Yeah, you too.

ETHAN. What's that?

HAMPTON. It's a head in a bag.

ETHAN. *(beat)* Nice. *(beat)* Where's everybody else?

HAMPTON. Shana and Daniel are in the backyard playing Frisbee. Earl is…not sure. *(beat)* You look good.

ETHAN. Been doing roadwork around Myrtle Beach.

HAMPTON. Myrtle Beach. Good eating down there?

ETHAN. Here and there. Once spring break hits, though…

(*Enter* **SHANA** *and* **DANIEL***. A moment.* **SHANA** *embraces and kisses* **ETHAN***. Then she slaps him.*)

SHANA. Where the hell did you go!?! Why haven't I heard from you!?! *(embracing)* I hate you. You're a complete idiot. *(slapping)* You stay away for two months without so much as a PHONE CALL!?! WHAT IS *THAT!?!* *(embracing)* God, I missed you. Don't you ever do that again.

ETHAN. Okay, just stop hitting me, all right?

SHANA. Are you staying? If you say you're leaving, I swear to God I'll fuck you up!

(ETHAN *whispers something into* SHANA*'s ear.* SHANA *exits to bedroom area.* ETHAN *looks at* DANIEL.)

ETHAN. You can talk now, Daniel.

(DANIEL *rushes to* ETHAN *and embraces him tightly.*)

DANIEL. Hi! We missed you, Ethan!

ETHAN. Me too, kid. *(beat)* So, how are things?

HAMPTON. Things are good. You know –

ETHAN. Oh, you don't have to tell *me.* Not a day goes by where I don't read about you in the paper or see you on TV. I almost feel as if I *really know you.*

HAMPTON. Yeah, yeah, it's all a big joke, so –

ETHAN. Is it a *joke* now? I don't remember laughing.

HAMPTON. Not laughing *ha ha*, but –

DANIEL. What's in the bag?

ETHAN. *(beat)* I brought presents.

(DANIEL *goes for the bag,* ETHAN *playfully slaps his hand away.* ETHAN *pulls out a ball cap.*)

This is my official *Team Vamp* baseball cap, one size fits all.

(ETHAN *pulls out a bumper sticker.*)

That's my "Hampton for President" bumper sticker. If I ever get a car, that's going right on.

HAMPTON. I didn't authorize this…

(ETHAN *pulls out a T-shirt.*)

ETHAN. Oh, I love this one. "I was bitten by a vampire, and all I got was this lousy T-shirt."

HAMPTON. You've completely lost your mind, haven't you.

ETHAN. Oh, wait…this is my favorite. I save the best for last.

(ETHAN *pulls out Ken and Barbie dolls.*)

ETHAN. Vampire Ken and Victim Barbie!

(ETHAN *starts doing a little show with them.*)

ETHAN. The Barbie is supposed to squirt blood from her

neck. It never works right. *(beat)* You're really onto something here. The stores are flooded with vampire paraphernalia. It's a consumer bonanza. You can get vampire toothbrushes, lipstick, coasters, toilet paper – anything! And all these little buyers and sellers know who you are, love what you are, and would love to be what you are. You have become a hero...no, better than that...you have become a caricature. Dare I say...a *myth?* Congratulations. You're a celebrity. You have become...and *believe me*, the irony does not *escape* me...a consumable item.

HAMPTON. Hey listen, man, it was really easy to be a *rumor* once upon a time. Even the hysterics of vampire epidemics in Eastern Europe didn't last long. Technology is catching up. And people like you and Earl – *especially* Earl – you're one surveillance camera away from exposure.

ETHAN. Never should have told you that vampires could be seen in mirrors and on camera.

HAMPTON. How long did you think I wouldn't be able to deduce simple physics?

ETHAN. I was hoping for another hundred years or so. Figured I come up with some other excuse when the time came.

HAMPTON. No seriously – the mystic element? We're not *invisible* – not *air* – what the fuck?

ETHAN. You are the master of the redirect.

HAMPTON. Oh, are we having *that* kind of conversation? Fine – what would you like to talk about? I know! Let's talk about geography – sound good? *(beat)* Hell, we've been in this town for *years* now, right? Because *nothing ever happens here*. Except murder. Lots and lots of murder.

ETHAN. Care to tell me what the fuck this has to do with anything?

HAMPTON. Admit it, man, you felt it as much as I did,

and that's why we've lived here longer than any other place. Because you were scared of what was coming for us. So, what was next on your agenda? Pig farmers in Nebraska? Live with the aborigines in Australia? Well, no thanks. At least I had sense enough to make a move toward the oncoming threat, instead of running from it.

ETHAN. Really? *Denial?* That's your angle?

HAMPTON. I don't know what you're talking about.

ETHAN. Do you want to be one of them again but *better?* Because you're on your way. I've been witness to the progress from the get-go. Two hundred years ago, you jumped out of trees toward the smell of a guy on a horse and got him every single time. One hundred years ago, you got it into your head that going after fat drunk guys would be easier. Seventy-five years ago, you started shooting fat drunk guys with a shotgun – which you claimed was for sport. And about twenty years ago, you got us a remote control.

HAMPTON. I was working within the changing times, and so were you, I thought.

ETHAN. After all this time, you want to become a slave?

HAMPTON. Slaves don't make the kind of money I do.

ETHAN. That's because if they have enough money, they don't realize that *that's* what they *are.*

(SHANA *enters with two suitcases.*)

HAMPTON. I'm not saying it doesn't have its pitfalls, but –

DANIEL. What's going on?

ETHAN. I came to get you and Shana and Earl, Danny. We can still hide you, kid. I have a house in South Carolina. A good-paying job and everything. It's nice and peaceful. They even have a zoo.

DANIEL. *(beat)* Can Hampton come?

ETHAN. *(beat)* He doesn't want to come. And there's nothing I can do about that.

DANIEL. *(pause)* I can't come either. I'm on the committee.

ETHAN. Yeah, all right. *(to* **HAMPTON***)* You had better take care of him.

HAMPTON. *(beat)* In a hundred years, we're gonna sit back and have a good laugh about all this.

*(***DANIEL** *grabs hold of* **SHANA***.)*

DANIEL. Will you visit us?

SHANA. Of course, sweetie.

*(***SHANA** *lets go of* **DANIEL***.* **HAMPTON** *approaches her with his arms out. She grabs her suitcases.)*

SHANA. Can we just do this, please?

*(***SHANA** *exits.* **ETHAN** *gives* **DANIEL** *a piece of yellow memo paper.)*

ETHAN. That's our address and phone number. You give that to Lord Evido when he comes home.

*(***DANIEL** *nods.* **ETHAN** *exits.* **HAMPTON** *sits on the coffin.* **DANIEL** *sits in the recliner. A moment. The girls enter.)*

GRETCHEN. *(beat)* It was quiet, so we thought…where's Ethan?

DANIEL. He's gone. Shana too.

LUCINA. Shoot. There goes our feel-good story.

TRESA. You know what I was thinking? That we need a song of solidarity.

LUCINA. You mean like "We are the Champions"?

TRESA. Yeah! *(beat)* Except not that one, obviously.

LUCINA. I suppose "We Shall Overcome" is out of the question?

GRETCHEN. A Negro Spiritual hardly makes sense.

TRESA. We need something with pizazz, you know? Something modern.

LUCINA. Something we can dance to.

GRETCHEN. No dancing.

LUCINA. Don't be such a poop, Gretchen.

(**HAMPTON** *turns on his recorder.*)

HAMPTON. *(to recorder)* One of the things I really hated about being human…was that people I loved would die. Being a vampire means that people only leave. *(beat)* Right now…I don't know which is worse. *(beat)* What's that number, Danny? *(looks around)* Where's my phone? Anyone seen my phone?

(Enter **EARL** *through kitchen.)*

GRETCHEN. Oh, good. Just the man I wanted to see. Let's talk, Earl.

EARL. I am not Earl.

GRETCHEN. Oh, I'm so sorry, *Earl.* Everyone seems to call you *Earl,* so I must be mistaken when I call you *Earl.* So tell me, *Earl,* just what the hell do you think you're up to? The Christy Banks *incident?* The Vanruegen *incident?* Do you enjoy having to see Hampton have to deal with so much? I mean, he's a wreck. Is that what you want, *Earl?* To see him crash and burn – because at the rate you're going, you could single-handedly bring this movement to a grinding halt. And then what are we left with? If you're not *with* us then you're *against* us, *Earl.*

HAMPTON. Gretchen.

GRETCHEN. I could simply go to the police and give them a description of a vampire, dressed in a black cape, unable to join the *timeline.* With or without you, this movement continues. So, what say we play ball, *Earl?* We'll go out right now and get you some fancy duds. Something casual, I'm thinking. Nothing too bright, because I'm thinking that you're a "winter". That way you and I can have a conversation without me thinking I'm talking to a movie screen. ARE YOU LISTENING TO ME, *EARL!?!* OR ARE YOUR EARS TOO OLD TO HEAR ME!?!

DANIEL. DON'T YELL AT HIM!

GRETCHEN. Let me handle this.

DANIEL. YOU STOP RIGHT NOW!

GRETCHEN. Don't raise your voice to me, Daniel.

DANIEL. DON'T TELL ME WHAT TO DO!

GRETCHEN. GO TO YOUR ROOM, YOUNG MAN!

(EARL grabs GRETCHEN by the ponytail and pulls her up so that she is on her tiptoes.)

LUCINA. Put her down.

EARL. *(to GRETCHEN)* You speak frequently. You should not.

GRETCHEN. Is this any way to treat a lady!?! Get out of the Dark Ages, Vlad!

LUCINA. I'm very serious, Earl. Don't you dare hurt her.

(A moment. EARL pushes GRETCHEN closer to DANIEL. A moment.)

EARL. Apologize.

GRETCHEN. Excuse me very much?

EARL. Apologize to Daniel.

GRETCHEN. *(reluctantly)* I'm sorry I yelled at you, Daniel.

LUCINA. There, she said it. Now put her down.

GRETCHEN. What!?! I apologized! *(pause)* I shouldn't have yelled at you that way, Daniel. I'm very, very sorry. I should never yell at you.

(EARL lets GRETCHEN go. LUCINA and TRESA advance, but GRETCHEN stops them.)

GRETCHEN. The last thing we should do is fight among ourselves. Let's just get back to work.

(The girls confer as EARL approaches DANIEL and HAMPTON.)

EARL. *(beat)* It is a good night to hunt. *(beat)* Perhaps you and Daniel should join me.

HAMPTON. Uh…maybe later. I got some stuff to think about. *(beat)* Thanks, though. *(beat)* Seriously, has anyone seen my phone around anywhere?

EARL. Daniel?

(**DANIEL** *clenches the yellow piece of paper in his hand.*)

DANIEL. I...I want to but...Do you like it here with us, Lord Evido? I mean, you wouldn't want to...you know?

EARL. I do not understand, Daniel.

(**DANIEL** *puts the piece of paper into his pocket.*)

DANIEL. Never mind. *(beat)* I'm not really hungry. I would hunt, but I'm not really hungry.

EARL. *(beat)* Very well. *(beat)* Feast while you can, my brothers.

(**EARL** *exits through the front door.*)

GRETCHEN. *(beat)* Seriously, Hampton, if he won't leave, then maybe you should consider moving. We should have enough money to move out of this shithole.

TRESA. Some nice college town?

GRETCHEN. We have almost full support of most of the youth culture, so why not?

HAMPTON. Earl's right. You talk a lot.

(**LUCINA** *starts rubbing* **HAMPTON**'*s shoulders.*)

LUCINA. We just need to not be tense. Ooo, you're all knotted up, baby.

TRESA. *(beat)* Fuck it. Let's just kill him. Hang him up by his own bloody cape.

(**HAMPTON** *removes* **LUCINA**'*s hands from him and stands up. A moment.*)

HAMPTON. Let's go, Danny.

(**HAMPTON** *and* **DANIEL** *head for the front door.*)

Hang out – or don't – whatever. We're just gonna maybe hunt for a while. You heard the man..."feast while you can." Can I bring anyone back anything?

(**HAMPTON** *doesn't wait for an answer and shuts the door behind them. Light change.*)

Scene Thirteen

(Enter **ETHAN** *and* **SHANA**. *They sit on their suitcases.* **HAMPTON** *and* **DANIEL** *enter on the other side. The girls continue to lounge about.)*

ETHAN. I would have booked a flight but my credit card is maxed out. Should only be five or six trips to get there.

SHANA. We shouldn't have left. We should have waited for Evido – tried harder with Danny.

DANIEL. I think maybe Evido would go to that one forest he likes to go to.

HAMPTON. Well, whatever, I'm tired of looking for him.

TRESA. How about "Bridge Over Troubled Waters"?

GRETCHEN. Too hippie.

ETHAN. He's got the address.

SHANA. It doesn't feel right.

DANIEL. We shouldn't be here. Something's wrong.

HAMPTON. Calm down. Everything's fine.

LUCINA. "Let it be"?

GRETCHEN. Christian reference.

ETHAN. Give it a bit. Maybe Evido can talk Danny into coming down.

SHANA. You're not going to leave, are you?

ETHAN. Nope.

SHANA. Because you did before.

ETHAN. Won't happen again.

DANIEL. I don't wanna do this anymore.

HAMPTON. Fine, we'll go home.

DANIEL. No, I mean, I wanna go with Ethan and Shana. And Evido can come.

*(***HAMPTON*** notices something offstage and behind him.)*

HAMPTON. Okay, good – we'll talk about it.

TRESA. "Instant Karma".

LUCINA. It's *not* a *Christian* reference.

GRETCHEN. I only know what I hear.

DANIEL. You should come too.

(**HAMPTON**'s *bad feeling increases. The sound of a mob starts to rise up.*)

HAMPTON. Sure thing, kid. Let's just – duck in here for a moment.

TRESA. "Sabbath Bloody Sabbath".

GRETCHEN. Now you're just being bitchy.

LUCINA. Well, we've been at this for hours, and you keep shooting down our ideas.

GRETCHEN. Only because, up to this point, they've all been *bad.*

DANIEL. I want you to listen to me, okay?

HAMPTON. I hear you, just –

(**DANIEL** *looks around and sees a mob closing in.*)

DANIEL. Who are they?

HAMPTON. Let's just –

TRESA. I give up. Bad idea. We don't need a song of solidarity.

GRETCHEN. Yes, we do.

LUCINA. What for?

GRETCHEN. Because we're trying to promote *unity, dammit!*

DANIEL. They want to hurt us.

HAMPTON. Not now, Danny.

DANIEL. I'm so hungry.

HAMPTON. Come on, kid, get a grip, we can –

(**DANIEL** *roars and runs offstage, as* **HAMPTON** *tries to hold him back.*)

HAMPTON. DANIEL! *Shit!*

(**HAMPTON** *bursts off after* **DANIEL**. *The mob sounds rise…*)

SHANA. I hate the bus.

ETHAN. Yeah, sorry.

*(The mob sounds stop abruptly. **ETHAN** gets a sudden sharp pain in his head that comes and goes.)*

SHANA. What was that?

ETHAN. Nothing. I'm probably just hungry.

(They exit. Blackout.)

Scene Fourteen

(GRETCHEN *paces,* TRESA *mourns. A moment.*)

GRETCHEN. This has got hate-crime written all over it. We'll call the media, then the governor! No! Media first! *Then* the governor! Then the police!

TRESA. Why him? Jesus Christ, of all people...

(LUCINA *enters.*)

LUCINA. I've calmed him down, but he's in a bad place right now.

TRESA. Do you blame him? Attacked in the street like that?

LUCINA. He wouldn't take a sedative, so –

TRESA. Like that's going to solve anything.

LUCINA. I don't see you trying to do anything to help!

TRESA. Right now I wanna kill somebody, okay!?!

(*knock*)

GRETCHEN. That kind of attitude will not fix anything!

(GRETCHEN *answers the door.* BILLS *and* SHARP *enter flashing their badges.*)

GRETCHEN. Did somebody call the police *already*?

BILLS. Good evening, ma'am. I am Detective Bills, and this is my partner Detective Sharp. Am I correct in assuming that this the residence of Hampton the vampire?

GRETCHEN. That's correct, and boy, does he have a story for you.

LUCINA. Wait. Why are you – what's this all about?

BILLS. We just need to take him downtown. Ask him a few questions.

SHARP. Nothing to worry about.

LUCINA. Ask him questions about what? About Daniel?

BILLS. (*referring to notepad*) Mr. Hampton has been connected with the deaths of eighteen individuals.

SHARP. Eighteen.

BILLS. That also includes seriously injuring twenty-one others.

SHARP. Three with minor injuries.

BILLS. And a whole lot of eye witness reports.

SHARP. So we want to get his side of the story.

BILLS. Standard procedure. That and…

SHARP. There is the whole Christy Banks thing.

BILLS. But that's a soft lead.

SHARP. Not an implication around.

BILLS. But he *knew* her.

SHARP. But that's neither here nor there.

BILLS. Nor here.

SHARP. A few moments of Mr. Hampton's time.

BILLS. That's all we ask.

TRESA. *(beat)* You're here to arrest him! He was defending himself from a mob! They killed one of ours! I'll bet you anything those eyewitness reports are from people who attacked them, *am I right?*

SHARP. Just watch the hostility, ma'am.

TRESA. Hostility? Do you want to see hostility?

GRETCHEN. Tresa, please! Lucina? Would you please go get Hampton?

(**LUCINA** *exits to bedroom area.*)

GRETCHEN. We are perfectly willing to cooperate, gentlemen, but please try to understand that, as we've been told the story, it appears that this is a cut and dry case of self-defense.

SHARP. That's what we're trying to establish.

BILLS. Can I get your names, please?

GRETCHEN. Of course. I am Gretchen, this is Tresa, and the other one is Lucina.

SHARP. And your last names?

GRETCHEN. Van Horn.

BILLS. All three of you?

GRETCHEN. Blood relation, yes.

(*Enter* LUCINA.)

LUCINA. He's gone. I can't find him. The window's open…

BILLS. Would you mind if we had a look around?

SHARP. Just to be sure.

BILLS. We like to be sure.

SHARP. That's the job.

BILLS. Not that we don't trust you, but…

SHARP. We don't trust anybody.

GRETCHEN. Of course.

(BILLS *and* SHARP *pull out their guns.*)

GRETCHEN. Uh…that won't be necessary, sirs.

BILLS. You never know about these things.

GRETCHEN. No, I mean…the weapons…never mind.

BILLS. I carry my peace of mind in this gun, lady.

SHARP. He does.

(BILLS *and* SHARP *exit into the kitchen.*)

GRETCHEN. (*beat*) I think we're going to need a lawyer. A really good one. I'm not saying we should, but if you two happen to find one…bite him. You didn't hear that from me.

(BILLS *and* SHARP *enter.*)

BILLS. Make a mental note of that.

SHARP. On it.

(BILLS *and* SHARP *exit to hallway.*)

LUCINA. Pro bono probably won't do at this point. I can't believe how –

(*Screaming and gunfire heard off. The girls run off toward the noise. A moment. The girls enter.*)

This is really going to look bad.

(HAMPTON *slowly brings up the rear. He is bloody and his clothes torn into tatters.*)

GRETCHEN. Jesus *Christ*, Hampton! After all the work we've done...all the commitment...all the friggin' *money*, you decide that you want to start eating authority figures!?! What were you thinking!?!

HAMPTON. *(beat)* I don't want to think. I just want to remember.

GRETCHEN. *(beat)* Hampton? Hampton? *(beat) Dammit!* He's going primal on us!

LUCINA. Well, *do* something!

(GRETCHEN *slaps* HAMPTON. *A moment.*)

HAMPTON. *(strangely complacent)* Hi.

GRETCHEN. Are you back, Hampton?

HAMPTON. *(beat)* Yeah...yeah, I'm fine.

GRETCHEN. Great. Now, what you just did? That?

HAMPTON. You mean ripping the throats out of those two cops? Yeah, I did that. Felt *really good.*

GRETCHEN. Listen to me, Hampton. We're not talking about a simple PR move here to blanket tracks. We're talking about a full-on cover up.

TRESA. *(beat)* They never showed up. That's the story. They may have been *supposed* to come over, but they never showed up.

GRETCHEN. Keep thinking along those lines. Oh God, this is a nightmare.

LUCINA. We have to drain the bodies completely, you know. Maybe bury them. We can't just stick them in the fridge like normal.

GRETCHEN. Did they touch anything? We'll have to scrub this place down. And while we're doing that, we can come up with a new plan of attack.

HAMPTON. *(giddy)* A new plan of attack? And what might that be? To just give in? I'm all for that. Let's go to work for the government, or become circus acts, or whatever we need to put us in our place. Why not? At least we're alive, right? And what's better than living? Sure, we can surrender our lives...but at least we're happy living in freedom. Sign me up for that.

GRETCHEN. You know damn well that we were making progress.

HAMPTON. Because I got enough television exposure to put a nice, sweet face to the fear of being devoured? Hey, look, it's Hampton the successful vampire! He may eat us, but at least he'll be nice!

GRETCHEN. *(beat)* Okay, what you're doing right now? It's called *venting*. We've *all* had a hard night. We all grieve for Danny. But let's come to an agreement, okay? Whatever it is rippling through your unthinking little head right now? You are not to go on television with these ideas –

HAMPTON. I KNOW HOW THE BOOK IS SUPPOSED TO END!

(**HAMPTON** *suddenly grabs his recorder.*)

HAMPTON. A new plan of attack! Revolution! Disruption of the powers-that-be! The *digestion* of the moral major-ity! Play ball!?! Fine! Play *this* ball! Come to our field! Accept that the world was not created for *you!* Now more than ever, belong to the futility! Let we, the vam-pires who inhabit the world, show you the way! Learn humility through us! For we will eat you regardless of country, color, or creed! Are you a good Christian? Line starts to the left! Are you a Jew? A Muslim? A Buddhist!?! Don't argue, you'll all have your turn! But to be fair, we must first concentrate on those who think that they can save themselves by contributing to the cause…*(beat)* "Please, Mr. Vampire, don't kill me, I have a lovely life, and a child and wife, and a dog, and a garden! I donated money to the fight." Oh, I'm sorry, thanks for playing. Because at the end of the night, if someone's just hungry, then that's bad luck for you, my friend. *(beat)* Death to the Imperialist Anglo-Saxon cows that graze on greener grass! Let them be plump and stupid so that we may suck the life out of their wobbly cow heads! Let them toss money, power, and influence at our teeth as we tear into their pathetic little hides and find the truth of their existence in the sweet gush of blood! Create vampires out of the oppressed! Give the meek the means to inherit the Earth! Build an army out of the wretches who linger about this life, deformed only by societal watermarks! Together we will feast on the power, ripping the throats out of any government that opposes us! And create a new government...A new government...to govern vampires...whose up for that task? Would they be any better? Probably not. They wouldn't even have to be real...they could have push-button faces...vibrating corpses...old men tied in electrical knots...capable of nothing but repeating the history behind them...

GRETCHEN. Hampton? I know that you're really sad right now because of Daniel. But you're really freaking out right now, and I think maybe we should sit down and talk about this.

HAMPTON. *(beat)* We used to be people's deepest, darkest fears. The one they never spoke about because they only wanted to believe that such things only existed in pages of books, or on television, or on the big screen. They could never *believe*, because it was all too much. And now? Now...nothing...Now, we see the path we follow. We stand at the threshold of a ruined civilization. Consumed by us. Until there is nothing left to feed on. *(beat)* We are the dead gods. And they just found out that we existed. That we are real. *We are real.* **(HAMPTON** *looks at his recorder. A moment.)* *(chuckling)* How about that? My batteries are dead.

*(A high-pitched noise begins. The vampires grab hold of their ears. The **HUNTER** enters the door holding the device that emits the noise. The vampires collapse and wail. Blackout.)*

Scene Fifteen

(**HAMPTON, GRETCHEN, LUCINA,** *and* **TRESA** *are all dead.* **EARL** *enters as he did in the first scene. He examines the bodies until he comes to* **HAMPTON***. The* **HUNTER** *enters from the kitchen. He turns on his flashlight and examines* **EARL***.*)

HUNTER. If you're dressed up for Halloween, you're about two months early.

(The **HUNTER** *approaches* **EARL***.* **EARL** *remains still.)*

Ready for the big screen, I'd say. See kids like you all the time. Dressin' up like vampires, pretendin' to like drinkin' blood – doesn't vary much from state to state. You come to get yourself authenticated? That it? *(beat)* What's your name?

EARL. *(pause)* Earl.

HUNTER. Well, Earl, bein' a vampire ain't all about that slicked back hair and campy cape. All it is, is an excuse for somebody like me to exterminate somethin' like them. It's my job…my *callin'* you could say, to eradicate these parasitical bastards and send them back to the Hell that shit'em out. *(beat)* All the political equality talk? Just a bunch of smoke. Got a new idea in their heads. Make themselves a part of the culture, eat their way from the inside out. As bad as Communists, except worse, cuz Commies don't drink your blood, just your minds. *(beat)* Can't have the enemy know all the tricks of the trade, can you? Can't imagine what would happen if they knew about all my little toys.

(The **HUNTER** *holds up the device.)*

This thing belts out a sound so high that only vampires can hear it. Higher than dogs, or any animal you can say. I just press this little button right here, and humans walk on by. Vampires? They look like they're havin' seizures. Disrupts'em somethin' fierce. Got this from an old hand down in Mississippi, where vampires are ripe. Don't remember what it was like huntin' them down before.

(The **HUNTER** *holds the device out toward* **EARL** *and clicks it on. It is broken.)*

Unfortunately, this guy...*(kicks at* **HAMPTON***)* this piece of shit right here...he managed to bust it up pretty good. These things are a bitch to fix, let me tell ya. *(beat)* There was talk of outlawin' me. I just went about my business, lettin' people sleep their little sleeps, while I was out there savin'em. So what happens? Well, if vampires exist, then vampire hunters must exist. And suddenly there's this...whaddya call it...a government sanction, sayin' that you gotta have yourself a permit to hunt vampires. Now, don't get me wrong, I am in full support of the government of the United States of America, but when they start wanting the citizens to ask for permission to hunt down serious threats? Then that's when I got a problem. The Bill of Rights? That's for human beings, and these things ain't human. You wanna make it illegal? That don't mean you can stop me from puttin' an end to these feeders. You can talk to me about niggers and wetbacks and faggots and Islams all you want, but I know the true face of evil. *(beat)* You may think that becoming a vampire is cool or hip, and everybody's doin' it – a way to cheat ol' Mr. Death...but be forewarned, *Earl.* Mr. Death don't have favorites. He knows, like I know, that behind every door is a guy just like me...holding your fate in a sharpened piece of wood.

(The **HUNTER** *slowly heads for the front door.)*

In my line of work, either there's a job well done, or nothin' at all. *(beat)* Have a good night, Earl.

*(***EARL** *quickly grabs the* **HUNTER** *by the throat and pulls him down, devouring him. A moment.* **EARL** *stands up, looks around the room. He pulls out the bright green pamphlet and tosses it away. He looks around one last time and exits through the front door, leaving it open.)*

(A moment. **HAMPTON** *raises his hand and drops it.)*

(Spot on **ETHAN** *and* **SHANA**. **SHANA** *has her arms around* **ETHAN**, *her face sadly pressed against him.)*

ETHAN. *(with unfortunate irony)* Vampires kill humans to survive. They live off the blood of others. They kill because it is necessary. They do not discriminate. They have no religion. They have no faith. Blood is necessary to them. The blood of humans. It gives them power. They kill because it is pleasurable. They care nothing for humans. They are *not* human. They exist to promote evil. They *are* evil. There is no sense of decency within them. There is no mercy. They have no emotions. They have no loyalty. They have no sense of family. They have no capacity for compassion...morality...love.

END

CPSIA information can be obtained
at www.ICGtesting.com
Printed in the USA
BVHW07s1253080918
526909BV00002B/65/P